Angela Huth has written three collections of short stories and seven novels, including *Nowhere Girl, Virginia Fly is Drowning, South of the Lights, Invitation to the Married Life* and *Land Girls*. She also writes plays for radio, television and stage, and is a well-known freelance journalist, critic and broadcaster. She is married to a don, lives in Oxford and has two daughters.

By the same author

Fiction
Land Girls
Nowhere Girl
Sun Child
South of the Lights
Wanting
Invitation to the Married Life
Monday Lunch in Fairyland and other stories
Such Visitors and other stories
Another Kind of Cinderella

Non-Fiction
The English Woman's Wardrobe

For Children
Eugenie in Cloud Cuckoo Land
Island of the Children (ed)
Casting a Spell (ed)

Plays
The Understanding
The Trouble with Old Lovers

Virginia Fly is Drowning

ANGELA HUTH

An *Abacus* Book

First published in Great Britain by William Collins & Sons 1972
This edition published by Abacus 1995
Reprinted 1995, 1996 (twice)

A CIP catalogue record for this book is available from the British
Library.

ISBN 0 349 10672 X

Printed and bound in Great Britain by Clays Ltd, St Ives plc.

Abacus
A Division of
Little, Brown and Company (UK)
Brettenham House
Lancaster Place
London WC2E 7EN

For
Patricia Strachan
my sister

Chapter 1

Virginia Fly was raped, in her mind, on average twice a week. These imaginings came at no particular time of day: she was never prepared for them and yet never surprised by them. They vanished as quickly as they came, and left her with no ill effects. One moment there would be this glorious vision of a man's hand running down the length of her body, causing the kind of shiver down her spine that sent her fingers automatically to do up the three buttons of her cardigan, and the next minute she would hear herself saying, with admirable calm,

'Miranda, I think it's your turn to wipe the blackboard.'

The real dreams, however, the night-time dreams, were another matter. These clung to her in the morning. Fragments of vivid scenes chafed her mind while she struggled to concentrate on the subject in hand. They soured her day.

This Friday had been one of those blighted days. The man with the black moustache – he seemed to be becoming one of the regulars – had torn at her flesh and uttered curses, or war cries, or screams of passion – she could not precisely decipher which – in a language she did not understand. Then he had left her on a cold slab of mud at the edge of a lake. There someone shook her and she half woke.

'Help me up! I'm so cold.' She could see in her mind the picture of herself, still, black hole of a mouth moving, muddy hair lashing across her face as she writhed about searching for elusive warmth.

'There, there. All your bedclothes off again.' Her
mother was chivvying about the room, pecking at the
curtains with her neat little wrinkled hands – snip,
snip, and the daylight bulged in, flat and grey. 'Your
father and I such tidy sleepers, too. Breakfast's on the
table.'

Breakfast was on the table every morning by the time
Mrs Fly came to wake her daughter. It was one of Mrs
Fly's little ways – little 'standards' as she called them.
Virginia was such a clever girl, always had been, all those
scholarships in art and what-not, but there were some
things a mother was always better at, weren't there, and
no daughter should ever forget them. Mrs Fly may not
have possessed much of an intellect, as she would be the
first proudly to admit, but she scored where Virginia was
weak – around the house. And every morning the small
private triumph of breakfast being on the table, before
Virginia was even awake, never lost its sweetness. The
small pleasures of life, as Mrs Fly often repeated to Ted,
were the ones that counted for her. Virginia, who was
always referring to one poet or another, once said Words-
worth put it rather well. Something about little nameless,
unremembered acts of kindness and of love, although in
the case of Mrs Fly they were hardly nameless and never
allowed to be forgotten.

While Mrs Fly revelled in life's small pleasures, her
husband Ted was content with more average ones. Indeed he was obsessed by life's averages and struggled
daily to keep close to them. He sat now at his bowl of
cereal and boiled egg – a nice average breakfast – reading
the *Daily Mirror*, soon to pass on to the *Daily Mail*, so as to
get a balanced view of the news. He looked up when his
daughter came into the room. A sallow girl, he thought,
privately. Not one to make the best of herself. Why did
she always have to scrape her hair back in that way, and

couldn't someone tell her to rouge her cheeks? She wore a long brown cardigan, flecked with rust, over a matching brown skirt. Drab, thought Mr Fly, hating the disloyalty in his own heart. He supposed they were the right sort of things to wear as a teacher, but he liked a bright colour himself, and Virginia was never very bright, even when she went out with the professor.

'You look like the end of a bad summer,' he said, fondly. 'Bad dreams?'

'I knew we shouldn't have had that cheese last night,' said Mrs Fly, chipping away at her egg in a way that both her husband and daughter found maddening. 'You know what cheese does to Virginia. It never has agreed with her.'

Virginia's mouth tightened, as it always did when she hadn't the energy to disagree. Her father noticed and quickly returned to reading his paper. His sensitivities were somewhat above average when it came to bristling atmospheres, and he didn't like them. There had been quite a lot in this house, lately, too.

Mrs Fly only noticed that her daughter was unusually quiet.

'No letter from Charlie again to-day, then?' she said, fingering a pile of dull-looking letters beside her own plate. Another of her regular little scores was over the post. No letter for Virginia, one up to her. Though in a way, to be honest, she would have liked Charlie to write more regularly. His letters seemed to cheer Virginia.

'I had one only Friday, if you remember.' Virginia was cool.

'So you did. And then of course the posts from America. You know what they are.'

'When you've been writing to someone for twelve years, Mother, you don't worry if the letters aren't as regular as they once were. You trust each other. Besides,

9

there's not much point in his writing too often at the moment. He'll be able to *tell* me all the news, soon.'

Mrs Fly put down the cup of tea she had just picked up.

'He's coming over? After all these years? You could knock me down with a feather. Ted, did you hear that? Charlie's coming over. When did he tell you? Why didn't you tell us before?' Virginia's secrecy always puzzled Mrs Fly.

'Last letter,' said Virginia. 'He'll be here in a couple of months. A hotel near Piccadilly Circus, he's staying at.'

'*That*'s nice and central,' approved Mrs Fly. 'Trust an American to find something in the middle of things and he's never even set foot in London. That's why the Americans are the nation they are, I think.'

'Well, that's something to look forward to.' Mr Fly smiled at his daughter.

'Quite,' said Virginia.

Later, in the cold November classroom, she settled her pupils down to painting sunsets. Sunsets always kept them quiet, and she was in no mood for questions. She sat at her high, old-fashioned desk, her buttocks comfortable in the dips carved out for them in the wooden chair, and doodled with a red pencil. She had to clear her mind. Charlie was coming and that was good. She would try to think of Charlie. She knew what he looked like only from the Graduation Day picture he sent her twelve years ago; a rather small, blunt face with the kind of regular features that make you wonder why their regularity isn't more handsome: crew-cut hair, rather large ears, friendly grin. When they had first become penfriends they had written cautiously to each other. *I went into Croydon this afternoon*, Virginia remembered writing in the early days, *and saw a marvellous film*. She would go on to describe it in much detail, urging him to see it if ever it reached Utah. Nowadays she wrote in a more shorthand way. *London yesterday. London Philharmonic at the Festival Hall, Chinese food with my professor afterwards.* She had grown to confide in him – that is, she told him all she did, apologising often for the lack of adventure, but her thoughts she kept to herself.

Over the years she had received hundreds of letters from Charlie in his dreadful handwriting, green ink, thin airmail paper that made reading practically impossible. Unlike her he had soon developed into a great confessor, but like most indulgent confessors he lacked that intrinsic humour which makes confessions on a grand scale tolerable, and often of late Virginia found his letters quite dull, and would skip several paragraphs.

She had kept the news of Friday's letter from her parents because it had in fact caused her something of a shock. For years Charlie had been threatening to come to England, but each time the plan had evaporated. Virginia had always found herself disappointed, but for the last two years a curious relief, when the plans failed, had overcome her disappointment. She wanted to meet him, and yet she wanted not to be disillusioned by him. In her present mood she was happy to postpone the meeting for years, so when he had written saying the ticket was booked, the hotel was booked, and even a couple of theatres were booked (*and I'm hoping for a nice steak and kidney pie afterwards in Leicester Square*), she had felt a momentary clamminess about the hands. Still, that was only the first reaction. By now she was quite calm, and even looking forward to it. It should be a happy two weeks. They had so much in common, so much to discuss: through their countless airmail communications they had grown to know each other well.

Virginia looked up from her doodling to the bent heads of her pupils. They were a good class. She was fond of them.

Her eyes travelled round the room: the steamed-up windows, the big brown radiator that cackled so loud a protest if you turned its heat up that everyone settled for a lukewarm compromise; the lump of old man's beard in a milk bottle that Jemima White had brought Virginia from the woods – Charlie, she thought. Perhaps, with Charlie.

And then a kind of double exposure happened in her mind, and over the scene of the classroom, faintly imprinted, was the cold flat landscape of her dream where the rape had taken place. In the distance, a tall branchless tree. It turned into the raised arm of a child.

'Please, Miss Fly, are you all right?'

'Yes thank you, Louise.' She had always been a horribly observant child, though she couldn't paint at all. One or two other heads were raised. Virginia felt an uncontrollable flush crawling up her cheeks. 'Now get back to your work. It's nearly time.'

When school was over, Virginia decided to walk home. It was three miles, but she felt in need of the air. She put up her umbrella and set off through the suburban streets of the small town, yellowy in the late November light, and with relief turned off into the lanes. They were gloomy too, with their dull puddles and dripping hedges. Leafless trees were scratched minutely against the sky like the branches of trees on cheap calendars, and the rain thudded an irregular pattern of noise on to her umbrella. Virginia felt weary in spirit, and thought about sex.

She had first heard about it from Caroline, her schoolfriend, a very advanced girl, at nine, with pin-point breasts and wavy hair. Caroline had heard about it from her brother who had heard about it from a farmer's son. They were sitting in a tree one day, early summer, plucking petals from an illicit bunch of roses, with a view to making home-made rose water.

'Bet you don't know something I know,' said Caroline.

'What's that?'

'Well, just something about grown-ups. Or children, for that matter.'

'What?'

'Well, if a boy puts his thing into a girl, she'll have a baby.'

'Puts it where?' There was a long pause.

'Oh, almost anywhere,' said Caroline.

Virginia looked up from her petals, incredulous.

'Who says?'

'My brother. His friend has seen sheep doing it. One of them stands on its back legs, so there.'

Caroline was pregnant at fifteen, and two years later Virginia received her first kiss from a man she met in a pub in Wales. She was on holiday there with her parents, strictly chaperoned every moment of the day. The pub was the first she'd ever been to, and no sooner had she and her mother sat down to their tomato juices than this man was upon them. He had a beautiful sing-song voice, and pale carrot hair, and he told Mrs Fly endless jokes that made her point her finger at him and say 'Ooh, you are a one.' When Mr Fly joined them with his light ale the man suggested he should take Virginia to the church and back – no more than a five-minute stroll. It was a fine example of Norman architecture, he said. Virginia, keen on architecture at the time, was eager. Mr and Mrs Fly agreed no harm could come, and they set off.

Soon as they left the pub the man's jokes dried up. To make conversation, Virginia asked his name.

'Just call me Jo,' he said, grabbing her hand and leading her into the churchyard. 'Graves first.'

Virginia followed him to a dusky corner of thick trees and long grass, all charcoal shadows and huge slabs of pitted stone. Jo turned to her and pinned her shoulders to a tombstone made in the shape of a cross – the cross bar was the same height as her shoulders, and she could feel a crust of moss through her thin coat behind her back. Suddenly, she knew what was going to happen. Her heart was beating very fast, and the point of Jo's tongue was darting about the narrow slit of his mouth.

'Now let's have it, quick, darling,' he said. 'They said we've got five minutes.'

'Have what? I don't know what you're talking about.' Caroline had said you *lie down*.

'Come on. Give us a kiss for starters.'

He snapped his mouth over hers and thrust his eel-like tongue down her throat. His breathing was somewhat impaired by the fact that his nose was buried in her cheek, and his breath came in jerky, strangled groans. Virginia opened one eye and could see the huge forest of his flaming scalp. She could feel his whole body taut, his hips seemed to be batting against hers. Suddenly, just as an unimaginable pleasure began to creep over her skin, he growled like a disturbed dog and jumped back from her.

'Go on, go on,' she heard herself saying, and leaving her arms high, parted, along the stone cross. 'Please don't stop.'

'Five minutes up, dear.' He glanced at his watch, voice clipped, sweat on his forehead.

Virginia let her arms drop to her sides. She felt very cold.

'Nice piece of architecture,' said the man, turning towards the church tower and sounding jokey again. Virginia followed him back to the pub with shaking knees.

Some six years after that incident, Mrs Fly attempted to tell her twenty-three-year-old daughter the facts of life. By that time, Virginia's actual experience was only increased by one further kiss, from the village organist after a multiple christening, and one old finger running down her thigh in the tube – but she did at least know the facts. Caroline had three children by now and spared no details of their conceptions, attempted conceptions and the great climaxes of their births.

Mrs Fly knew none of this and braced herself for her duty one night when Ted was at the Rotary Club.

She took great pains to see that the whole evening was normal, that Virginia wouldn't guess anything was up. After a supper of macaroni cheese and baked apples, Mrs Fly took position in her favourite tweed armchair by the fire, and armed herself with a dishcloth full of holes to darn. Virginia, tired after a trying day at school, sprawled in the opposite armchair with *Sons and Lovers*. She hoped her mother didn't want to have one of her conversations.

'Virginia?'

'Yes?'

'You are a bookworm. – Oh, don't let me bother you if you want to read.'

'It doesn't matter.' Virginia put the book down.

'It's just that – well, I thought we ought to have a little talk.'

'Oh? What about?' Virginia wondered if the headmistress had been on to Mrs Fly again, like she had been last month, wondering why she was so pale.

Mrs Fly snapped off a piece of cotton between her teeth.

'Just you and me, you know.' She paused while she threaded the needle. 'I thought we ought to have a little talk about the facts of life.'

'Oh, those.' Virginia smiled. 'I don't think there's much you need tell me about those.' Mrs Fly gave a little jump, pricking her finger.

'You don't mean to tell me – ?'

15

'No, no. My virginity's still intact, if that's what you're asking.'

'You gave me quite a little turn, for a moment. I know they all do it, these days. But, you know, when you're a mother, you don't quite like to think of your own daughter . . .'

'I suppose not,' said Virginia. 'Same as you don't quite like to think of your own parents.'

Mrs Fly looked up at her daughter with shock in her eyes, but reacted calmly. Her original plan thwarted, with gallant spontaneity she decided to change her tactics.

'Well, there's obviously no need for us to go into technicalities – you probably know more about them than I do, what with all those books they have to-day.' She gave a small laugh. 'No, what I'd like to talk about is more the spiritual side. Nobody talks about that so much these days.' She wove her needle expertly in and out of the threads.

'What about it?' asked Virginia, to end a pause whose length indicated her mother had lost track.

'Well, dear, how can I put it? – What I'm trying to say is this. The, er, act, shall I call it, doesn't end when it's over.'

'Oh?' Virginia, for once, felt herself to be scoring.

'What I'd like you to know is, once you've experienced it, once you've been fulfilled, nothing is ever quite the same again.' She looked at her daughter with unusual severity. 'Quite dull girls have been known to radiate, once they have experienced love . . .' Virginia felt a hot stone of nausea rise in her throat. 'I mean, take your father and I. In the old days – I'll always remember experiencing quite a little after-glow.'

At the thought of her parents doing anything which would give them a little after-glow, Virginia got up, went to the lavatory and was very sick. It occurred to her briefly that her mother was either mad, drunk on fantasy, or had been too influenced by the romantic novels she endlessly read. Virginia knew for a fact that they never undressed in front of each other, never went into the bathroom when the other was in the bath, and turned off the television if sex came into the programme. Indeed, her own conception must have been pretty miraculous, she thought, and poured herself a small glass of neat whisky to try to abolish the loathsome thought of her parents' bodies flailing about in the dark.

By then Mrs Fly realised that her plan had gone wrong somewhere, and, when Virginia took her chair again, she changed the conversation to the planting out of bulbs.

When Virginia arrived home she found her father locking the garage doors on his mini van, a car he treated with a care quite out of proportion to its value. When he saw Virginia he began unlocking the door again.

'I'll run you into the station.'

'Don't bother. I can easily get the six o'clock bus.'

'It's no trouble.' He liked doing small things for her.

'Well, that would be kind.' She smiled at him, knowing he had secret hopes of the professor.

Indoors, in the warm steamy kitchen, she helped herself to a new baked scone and a glass of milk. Her mother was a good housekeeper and had managed to make their 1914 house – white stucco and Tudor beams on the outside – reasonably bright inside. 'A pleasantly average home,' her father called it. In fact, it was probably inhabited with more ornaments than the average house: hundreds of glass animals, china birds and miscellaneous souvenirs crowded every shelf and window ledge, so that it was dangerous to draw the curtains without extreme caution.

Virginia's bedroom Mrs Fly had had decorated one

weekend ten years ago as a 'surprise', which really meant she firmly believed there was no point in consulting someone else about something you were better at. The surprise was pink walls straight off a chart, and blue and white striped curtains with pink roses trailing across the stripes. A fluffy nylon rug by the bed, a picture of a storm at sea over the bed, and a narrow shelf running along one wall intended for glass animals – at which point Virginia had rebelled and put her paperbacks and the photograph of Charlie.

The lattice window looked on to a rather dismal strip of garden, balding with paving stones, thin grass growing round the edges. Each summer Mr Fly became increasingly provoked by the act of mowing, and covered up a bit more grass with a few more paving stones, saying it was the area that counted, not the greenness. Beyond the dark hedges of the garden were lumpish Surrey hills, bracken covered, spiked with gloomy pine trees. Virginia knew every inch of the view by heart. She had stared at it for hours over the years, watching it tinged with the gaudy golds and salmons of a semi-suburban sunset, or heaving in a storm, or covered with unprinted snow, or feeble spring sun. It had never become more cheerful, and yet she was fond of it.

She looked out of the window now, at the straight heavy rain, and realised she could not risk her Hush Puppies. Boots, she thought. Pink chiffon scarf, and a change of cardigan. The professor, always immaculate himself, never seemed to notice her clothes. He only cared that she was neither too warm nor too cool – that she was always comfortable.

Kicking off her wet shoes, she pulled the candlewick bedspread off her bed and lay down, legs apart. She had often, at the end of despairing days, lain in such a position, speculating on what she would do if a man appeared at the window, climbed in, and seduced her. She imagined she might make some small, formal show of protest, so that he would respect her, then give in wildly and happily. When it was all over she would get up, go over to the mirror and look disbelievingly at the sight of herself – dishevelled, pink, and glowing as she had never been before.

'Thank you very much,' she imagined she would say. 'Please come again, any time.'

The familiar daydream over, Virginia rose and went to the window, half to check that there really was no ladder and no man there. Then she went to the dressing-table and studied her reflection, unusually critical. With a sudden gesture of defiance she pulled off the elastic band that strained her hair back into a dull switch, and shook her head until the hair fell untidily about her shoulders. Then she dabbed her face, rather greasy from the long day, with a cloud of yellowy white powder, pinched her cheeks, and ran a beige lipstick over her mouth. 'That should surprise the professor,' she thought, smiling to herself, 'he won't recognise me.' She realised her timeless tweed coat and gumboots would somewhat minimise the effect, but she had nothing else, and anyhow they gave her a feeling of security.

In the car her father appraised her in his own way.

'What is it to-night?'

'Mozart piano sonatas.'

'You've got yourself up for them. I like your hair loose like that.' Virginia tossed her head silently. Mr Fly, for comfort's sake, returned to a pet theme. 'I did it back from the station to-night in exactly eleven minutes fourteen seconds. In these weather conditions, skiddy roads, that's not bad going, you know.' For twenty years he had been timing his journey to and from the station, for ever trying to work out a precise average. He had records in all weather conditions, traffic conditions and times of year.

'That's only a minute or so longer than average in the rain, isn't it?' replied Virginia, who knew most of the records by heart.

'One minute five seconds, to be exact. But then the tyres are a bit down. That accounts for it.'

'Oh.' Virginia looked at her father's long profile; the pale eyes clutched in a grip of lines, the grey hair neatly shaved over the skinny neck, the collar of the old Viyella shirt minutely darned, and she felt an unaccountable affection for him. She knew she had not fulfilled many hopes he had for her, and yet he never chided her. Just kept on hoping, in his quiet way.

'The professor hasn't been down for a long time.'

'No, not for ages,' she agreed.

'Your mother would be delighted to have him down to lunch any Sunday, you know.'

'I know.'

'He was so interesting last time about Salzburg.'

'He's an interesting man.'

'Well, I'd be pleased to meet him again, myself.' He turned on the windscreen wipers, clearing away the thick drizzle that had gathered over the view. Tall black trees now sharply lined the road. ' "Conifer county of Surrey",' he said to himself, quietly. (He had always been a Betjeman man.) 'We don't have a very adventurous life, do we, Ginny? I hope it's not too dull for you.'

'Oh no,' said Virginia, thinking again of the way the man with the black moustache had left her, 'I wouldn't want adventure.'

An hour and a half later Virginia met the professor outside the concert hall in Wigmore Street. He was waiting for her under his umbrella. At the sight of her damp bare head a look of concern crossed his face, but was

quickly replaced with one of mild surprise. She looked
quite different with her loose hair.

'Good evening, Miss Fly.'

'Virginia, Professor, please.' She smiled.

'Then I am Hans to you.'

Virginia and the professor had been meeting every four
or five weeks – according to concerts – for almost three
years now. Every time they met their relationship pro-
gressed a little, warmed a little towards the end of the
evening (he had only been once to lunch, and that had
not been an easy occasion), but the lapse of the next few
weeks drained that ease away again, leaving the sharp
formality with which they newly greeted each other.
However, they were both now accustomed to the pattern
of their reactions to one another, and although they
recognised that they must start off formally, they weren't
ill at ease.

They walked, as usual, a few paces to a high-class coffee
shop with low red lights. The professor ordered a Danish
pastry for Virginia, a slice of Sacher Torte for himself,
and two frothy coffees.

Virginia swung her hair. The gesture provoked the
professor out of his customary habit of making no comment on her appearance.

'It is the first time all these three years you have let it
loose,' he said.

'Yes,' said Virginia. 'It's the end of a significant day.'
In her heart she knew it hadn't really been a significant
day, just dismal, but she didn't want him to feel sorry for
her.

He didn't ask about the significance of her day, or indeed anything much about her life. In turn, she knew
little of him – at least, of the last twenty-five years in
London. About the first thirty years, in Vienna and Salzburg, she had heard a hundred vivid stories.

They had met on a train, Guildford to London. As they drew into the station, with infinite caution and politeness, so that she would not feel he was making any form of advance to her, the professor had asked her if she could tell him how long it would take to walk from Waterloo to the Festival Hall. It so happened that Virginia, weary of waiting for someone to ask her out, had begun going alone to concerts in London, and she was in fact on her way to the Festival Hall herself that night. So, feeling a little daring but at the same time utterly safe – he didn't look like a murderer and she wasn't in search of a seducer in those days – she suggested they should go together.

In return for her kindness, the professor bought her a cup of coffee in the interval, talked brilliantly about Mahler, was an arrogant but amusing critic of the performance, and took her address. A few weeks later he wrote her a formal note asking if she would care to go with him to Verdi's *Requiem* at the Albert Hall, and the pattern of their future began.

Back at the concert hall the professor bought Virginia a programme which she read with a touching enthusiasm from cover to cover. Later she would store it in the bottom drawer of her dressing-table, along with several dozen such others, and a pile of the professor's polite invitations. (He never telephoned.) These were the only tangible proof of the one constant, if unadorned relationship she had ever had with a man. – Letters from Charlie, despite the occasional paragraphs of lust which burst from him between girl-friends, were not the same.

The Mozart audience wasn't a colourful one, but it was prepared to be responsive. The pianist, a fat woman in a cross-over bodice satin dress, which did nothing for her bust or arms, pounded her way through the pieces with a lot of head shaking but little else. She insulted the sonatas, and this annoyed the professor.

'A thoroughly bad evening,' he muttered. 'A real disgrace. I'm sorry, Virginia.'

Outside, it was still raining and had turned very cold. 'Would you like a hot drink?' he suggested. 'There's time.'

Why, Virginia wondered to herself, was she the kind of girl to whom people always offered a hot drink rather than just a drink? What was it about her that stopped people imagining she could do with a double whisky? For the first time in her life, that cold November night, she turned down the idea.

'I'd like some brandy, please,' she said, swinging her hair again. The professor raised his eyebrows.

'Oh, you are wild to-night. Very well.'

They went to a warm pub, shadowy with amber light, and drank cognac in a corner. The professor appeared a little perplexed by the unusual situation.

'You are very jumpy to-night. You are not relaxed. It was the bad music?'

'No, no. It's just that – this sort of life, my present life, is coming to an end.'

'Oh?' His dark eyes were dignified, briefly hurt.

'Charlie's coming over. You know, my American penfriend. He'll be here in a couple of months. Maybe less.' She smiled to herself. 'I don't know how long it'll take. A week or so, I suppose, to sort things out. We know each other so well already – that won't be a problem. And then we'll go back and live in Utah.'

'You mean, you are planning to marry this Charlie?' The professor ordered himself another drink.

'Well, we haven't actually planned anything, but it seems to have become a kind of unspoken agreement over the years.'

'And what happens if it doesn't work out? If you and

23

this Charlie, it turns out you hate each other's guts?'
There was almost a snarl in the professor's voice. A tiny
triangle of high colour had appeared on each of his cheeks.
Virginia wrapped her hands round her glass. She felt
unusually warm.

'He is very handsome and has a very interesting life,'
she said, quietly. 'I think we will be very well suited.'

'Oh, you child,' said the professor. 'You dear child.'
He pulled his huge cloak closer round his shoulders,
although he couldn't have been cold. 'Now this has happened, I can tell you something. But first, let me wish you
every happiness.' He smiled formally, politely at Virginia.
She bowed her head. Nobody had ever wished her that
kind of happiness before. 'From time to time it has crossed
over my mind,' the professor was saying, 'that one day I
should make you a very honourable proposal. I have post-
poned the hour because I have always felt in my bones I
am not to be recommended as a husband. You could be
my daughter. I am not suitable. And yet, you do not have
to be suitable to be compatible, do you?' He smiled, his
handsome teeth widening across his face and causing
a reflex action of interlocking lines to shift round his eyes,
cheeks and mouth. 'However, it was always a good idea
to live with, and now at least I may be spared a refusal
from you.'

At this point, Virginia realised she was quite drunk,
because the importance of what he was saying skidded
across her mind with only half the impact it would have
made upon her had she been completely sober. She smiled
kindly, stupidly at the professor. She wanted to giggle, but
controlled herself.

'Dear Hans,' she said, 'I must catch the train.'

'Very well.' He followed her, taking her arm more
firmly than usual.

At the station, as was his custom, he saw her safely

into a carriage. Just before he left her a thought occurred to him.

'There's the Bach Choir coming up in a couple of months. You remember, we went last year and enjoyed it? I wonder, would you allow me to take both you and this Charlie?' Virginia was unconscious of the flicker of sarcasm in his voice.

'That would be lovely,' she said, the words still a little unsteady. 'I'm sure Charlie would enjoy that, although he doesn't know very much about music.'

The professor kissed Virginia's hand, raised his hat, and bowed – the ceremony he always performed when he left her.

'Then that would be my pleasure,' he said, and walked down the platform without looking back.

The carriage was cold. Rain slid faster and faster across the windows. Virginia took the programme out of her bag, unfolded it, and read it all over again. She had had many enjoyable evenings with the professor. She would miss all the regular music. Of course, she could take Charlie to concerts, but it wouldn't be the same. For some unknown reason she found tears coming to her eyes. Crossly, for something to do, she found another elastic band in her purse and scraped her hair back again. She began to wish she hadn't had the brandy.

Back at home she found the orange lantern glowing in the porch. It gave a nice welcome, as her mother said. It also gave a nasty glow to the rhododendron bushes that clustered near the front door, Virginia thought, for the first time. Strange how she had never noticed how ugly they were before.

In the kitchen her mother had set out, as Virginia knew she would, a mug, spoon, and a tin of drinking chocolate already opened. On the stove milk stood ready to boil in a saucepan, and against the saucepan was propped a note.

I have put milk ready for boiling in saucepan, it said. *Biscuits in usual tin. I have quite a little surprise for you in the morning. We're all going to be famous, hope you had a good evening. Love, Mother.*

Wearily, Virginia made herself hot chocolate, from habit rather than desire. She knew the nature of her mother's surprises. Probably they were to be interviewed by people doing a house to house survey on soap powders, or her mother had found another dreadful old picture which she had mistakenly taken to be a Rembrandt. Certainly the news of a surprise did not mean that there was any reason to look forward to the morning.

When she had undressed and brushed her hair fifty times, Virginia knelt by her bed. She said her prayers out loud, as she had done for twenty-five years, as her mother had taught her.

To-night, when she had been through all the family and friends she wanted blessed, and the request for the professor to be happy, she suddenly added, with a fervour that surprised her:

'And please God, about Charlie. – If it's your will he shouldn't want to marry me, then please God, make it your will that he should want to seduce me. That, I pray you.'

Chapter 2

'They want us on television,' said Mrs Fly, finally, over the washing-up next morning. She was confused by the fact that Virginia hadn't asked what the surprise was to be. She was a funny girl, in some ways, Ginny. None of the ordinary things seemed to excite her.

'Who want us on television?' Virginia had, indeed, forgotten all about the surprise.

'That Geoffrey Wysdom, you know. The one who does all the serious documentaries, true to life.' Virginia had heard of him, but as she rarely watched television she had never seen one of his programmes.

'Who does he want on his programme?' she persisted. Once again Mrs Fly seemed confused. She clattered some plates noisily in the bowl.

'Well, not so much us, your father and I. It's you they want, actually.'

'And what do they want me to do?'

'That,' said Mrs Fly with a sudden determination, probably caused by fear of breaking the point of the news, 'is what I'm going to leave the researcher to tell you. She came round here yesterday evening. That's what she said she was, a researcher. A very nice girl. Very quiet voiced. I said it would be all right for her to come round about eleven this morning. I said you'd be in, and might be able to help her . . .' Mrs Fly trailed off.

As it was Saturday morning there was no school, only a pile of essays to be corrected. Virginia went up to her room to make her bed. She had had a good night, no dreams, and felt light-hearted as ever she could hope to

feel on a dun-coloured winter morning with the prospect
of an empty weekend ahead. The television news, though
she would never admit it to her mother, caused a mild
flicker of anticipation within her. It was probably something to do with education; views on teachers' lousy pay,
perhaps. Well, she knew her subject. She could be fluent
about that, and the idea of cameras gave her no sense of
fear. In fact, it could be interesting. It could be a breaking
point in her life. Someone might see her, and invite her
permanently on to an educational programme or fall in
love with her, write to her care of the B.B.C.—*Dearest Miss
Virginia Fly, I saw you on the box the other night. I hope you
don't mind my writing but it seemed to me you are the girl I have
been looking for all my life* . . .

' Virginia firmly opened the first exercise book. *A bee and
a spotted elephant had a fountain and a rainbow. They went for a
walk in the forest and they saw some animals* . . . Red pencil in
her hand, the letter from the unknown viewer remained
faintly on her mind.

The researcher came promptly at eleven. Jenny, she
was called. Red curly hair, bad legs stuffed into trendy
boots, a friendly smile, and a peculiarly alert look about
her, as if she was all prepared to be interested instantly in
everything.

Mrs Fly suggested coffee.

'Oh how lovely,' said the researcher. 'That's just what I
need. If it's not too much trouble?' She looked out of the
window at the scrawny garden, the mildewing leaves on
the ugly paving stones. 'It's so lovely to get out of London,'
she said. 'That's one of the great advantages of my job.
You go all over England.' Virginia felt the girl must be
playing for time. She smiled helpfully.

'It must be an interesting job,' she said. Then a thought
struck her. 'How did you find me?'

'Oh, we have people who put us on to people. Contacts,

you know.' Jenny was professionally vague. She buried most of herself in a huge shabby handbag and finally emerged with a notebook. 'Now, why I'm here.' She gave a sympathetic, rather guilty smile. 'About our programme . . . I expect you've often seen it? You know the sort of thing we do? – '

'I don't, I'm afraid, no,' said Virginia. 'I don't often watch television.'

'Really?' Jenny failed to conceal her amazement. 'Most people have. I thought we'd become popular viewing.' She gave a gurgly sort of giggle at her own joke. 'Anyhow, our aim is to get ordinary people on to the screen, and get them to talk exactly as if they were in their own homes – which in fact they usually are. And the amazing thing is, you've no idea how fluent the man on the street becomes once he gets on to his troubles.'

'Troubles?' inquired Virginia.

'Well, I mean, that is, in cases where people are in trouble. I have to admit, most of our programmes deal with sociological problems.'

'I see. You're sort of welfare workers of the air,' said Virginia, and before Jenny could deny it, added, 'but I haven't any troubles.'

'Troubles? Well, no, of course you haven't.' Jenny twitched a bit, and tossed her frizzy red hair about, sensitivities rising. 'That's just *some* of the programmes. Others are just . . . explorations into human predicaments, or different outlooks, if you know what I mean.' She smiled again, so nicely that Virginia could not but feel warm towards her.

'How can I help you?' she asked. 'Teachers' pay? I can tell you a lot of illuminating stories about that.'

'Well, no, nothing to do with being a teacher at all, as a matter of fact,' replied Jenny, who found approaching some of the stupider of the working classes a great deal easier than dealing with people with any intelligence. 'What we are doing, simply, is making a programme about, um, pre-marital love. Love to-day. Does it still exist? If so, how? That sort of thing.'

Jenny gave another dazzling, relieved smile. She had got the most difficult part of the explanation out. In return, Virginia looked at her wryly.

'I don't think I'm at all the person to help you,' she said. 'I think your contacts have misinformed you. I've never been in love. I haven't even got a boyfriend.'

'That's just why you *can* help us. You personify, if you like, the old-fashioned concept. You are – if you don't mind my saying so – a virgin, aren't you? And thirty-one, I think?' Virginia flicked her eyes in agreement. 'That's what I heard. Now, do you see where you come into our programme? We're going to talk to unmarried mothers in their teens, débutantes who've had abortions, ugly girls who can't find lovers, couples who are officially engaged for years and bust up – and so on. So you would fill the virgin gap, as it were. I mean, to-day, if you'll forgive me for saying so, there aren't many of them around. Your state of – intactness' (she knew when to flatter) 'is a rare one, to-day. Unbelievably interesting . . .' Jenny had got into her stride. The worst of the news was over. Virginia let her chatter on about the programme, about the great interest and indeed *help* the state of her virginity would be to millions of viewers, about how a few old-fashioned concepts about love still persisted to-day amid all the anarchy . . . All the time Virginia pondered.

'Geoffrey would be interviewing you himself,' Jenny was saying, with the air that Virginia would take this as a great compliment, 'there's no one like him to get people to talk.' She bit her lip, realising she'd gone too far.

'I'm afraid I've never seen Mr Wysdom,' said Virginia. 'But my mother watches his programmes.'

Jenny giggled conspiratorially.

'Well, I wouldn't watch telly either, actually, if it wasn't for the fact I was in it. We're supposed to keep in touch. Anyhow, how do you feel about it? Would you like a few days to think it over?'

'No thank you,' said Virginia, sharply, 'I'll do it.'

At that moment Mrs Fly came in with a tray of coffee. She turned to her daughter full of anticipation.

'Well, dear? What's the answer?'

'I've said I'll do it.' More dully, this time.

'Well, that is nice.' Mrs Fly always felt she had been denied some measure of fame. 'It *is* such a good programme, so honest. It's not as if they've asked you on one of those vulgar quiz shows, is it?' She laughed happily. 'You'll have to think about what to wear, being colour. No stripes, they say, don't they?'

'For heaven's sake,' said Jenny quickly to Virginia, 'don't give a second thought about what to wear. Just look like you do every day.' – I see, thought Virginia, she doesn't want me dressing myself up, climbing out of my drab virgin image. Right. I won't disappoint her.

'Will these things be all right?' she asked, mildly. Jenny closely observed her navy cardigan and skirt, the dark lacy stockings – the only frivolous thing about her – the pale cheeks and severely drawn back hair.

'Great,' she said, with an enthusiasm which Virginia wondered was strictly professional or wholly natural, 'absolutely great. Just look like that on the day.'

The day was the following Saturday. For a week the house had tingled with an air of expectancy conjured up by Mrs Fly. She had put all her energy into dusting, polishing, arranging and re-arranging the half-dozen rather tatty chrysanthemums that were left in the garden, and fussing

about whether everyone should have coffee in mugs or
Mr Wysdom should be given one of the best cups.

News of the invasion affected Mr Fly in a quiet way.
He walked about rather stiffly, that week, with a strange
quiet pride, only admitting to a close friend at work that
his daughter would be famous, now. Recognised for her
integrity. Virginia herself was calm, apparently little
interested.

Mrs Fly had seen to it the neighbours weren't unaware
of the event. Making the best of her reflected glory, she
made sure they knew the time the camera cars were expected. And indeed, when the time came, they did not fail
her. Virginia, peeping behind a curtain, noticed a certain
amount of restlessness in the nearby gardens: people
suddenly emerging at ten o'clock to pick a flower or to
search for an invisible milk bottle, and at the same time
give a quick glance up at number 14. This, felt Virginia,
was her mother's hour.

Jenny, followed by a cameraman and his assistant, a
sound recordist and lighting man, came with all the
equipment into the house. A tall pale man who said he
was what they called the director, then laughed, began
giving instructions. He ordered the furniture, that Mrs
Fly had spent hours arranging carefully the night before,
to be moved. But he was very nice about it all.

'You don't mind, Mrs Fly, do you? We'll put it all
back. But can we just *get rid* of that sofa and pull this armchair up here – and get rid of those flowers?' With each
idea he waved his long milky hands in the air like under-
water plants, and Mrs Fly said yes, of course, to everything.

Mrs Fly, eager to be helpful, tense from the sleepless
night the excitement had caused her, was shaking. She
had chosen to wear a hyacinth blue dress that glittered
in the dullest light, hardly suitable for a dank November

morning. Its deep boat-neck, trimmed with white cony fur, unkindly highlighted the rash of nervous pink patches that had flamed over her chest. Virginia had suggested that, considering the time of day, ordinary clothes might have been more appropriate. But Mrs Fly would not hear of any such thing. Television, after all, was almost like a party.

Mr Fly, for his part, sleeves rolled up, maty jokes with each member of the crew, kept getting caught up in all the wires and cables. At one moment he knocked over the tripod, and at another he fell over himself.

'I've always been interested in the technical side of things,' he said, as he struggled to his feet, trying to preserve some sort of dignity. Jenny, alert as ever, read an unseen message from the director's eye. 'His technical interest is a bloody nuisance,' it said. 'Get him out of here.' So Jenny suggested to Mr Fly they should retire to the kitchen. She did it with such tact that Mr Fly, had he been a less innocent man, might well have taken it as an overture to an especial relationship between them.

For most of the preparations Virginia stayed upstairs. At five past eleven she saw the arrival of a long silver car, out of which stepped the man who must be Geoffrey Wysdom. He wore a very wide-shouldered overcoat and leather gloves with holes punched in the backs. Walking up the path to the Flys' house he nodded at the neighbours in their gardens, and shouted a couple of good mornings with the ease of someone who is used to being recognised. No one replied.

Virginia went downstairs. Geoffrey Wysdom was taking off his coat but he stopped, half out of it, when he saw her.

'Ah! Hallo, hallo. I'm Geoffrey Wysdom. You must be Serena Fly.'

'Virginia.'

33

'Virginia, so sorry.' He held out his left hand, as his right was still in the overcoat sleeve, full of bonhomie. 'Are my lot nearly ready? Not causing too much confusion, I hope.'

Mr Fly and Jenny came out of the kitchen at that moment.

'Geoffrey Wysdom,' Mr Wysdom said quickly, to Mr Fly, before Jenny had a chance to introduce them. 'How are you, Mr Fly?' Then he bounced towards the sitting-room, took Mrs Fly's shaky hand, and established he was Geoffrey Wysdom once again.

When Geoffrey Wysdom entered the room, lit like a stage now, something recharged the atmosphere. Awe, respect, admiration, perhaps. He had about him an air of supreme self-confidence. He was full of merry quips and extravagant praise for the room, the furniture and the dreary garden outside. Sincerity shone from him. Mrs Fly thought he was wonderful, and he was quick to respond.

'Good heavens, Dresden, aren't they?' he asked her, pointing to a cabinet of china. Mrs Fly blushed.

'Well, no, not really Dresden,' she admitted, 'but just as precious to me.'

'I know quite a lot about china,' Mr Wysdom went on, 'in fact I'm something of a collector on the side. My wife and I have a marvellous collection at home.'

Virginia saw the director, who had stopped his directing by now, give a slight raise of one eyebrow towards Jenny, who concealed a smile. For a moment Virginia wondered if it had been old medals, or shells, in the cabinet, Mr Wysdom would have had a collection of those at home too. Perhaps it was all part of the putting at ease system: make the interviewee feel they have something in common with you, the man on the screen. But certainly he was doing a good job on Mrs Fly, anyway – congratulating her on her dress, her sofa and her curtains. She had almost stopped shaking, and the fiery red patches on her neck were beginning to fade.

Suddenly Virginia realised that the hubbub had died down. The room was empty of everyone but the cameraman, the sound recordist and the director, who for some reason chose to squat behind a rather small armchair, head bowed but still clearly visible.

Virginia was sitting on the sofa, ankles crossed, hands loosely together in her lap. Geoffrey Wysdom, opposite, was offering her a Turkish cigarette. All his smiles had disappeared, and now he no longer moved his mouth, it was hardly noticeable. Under the lights his hair, fraying slightly round the edges, was a greenish colour, and his high forehead glistened. In contrast to the glare of his wide, salmon pink tie, he looked very grave. Virginia had the impression that his eyes had become slightly damp.

From a long way away Virginia heard the quiet whirr of the camera, and part of the first question.

'. . . and so, as a teacher, how much chance do you have for a full social life?'

How much chance do I have for a full social life? Virginia smiled. Perhaps it would be this first smile that would win over the unknown viewer.

Dearest Miss Fly, when you smiled on television the other night I knew my life had changed . . . Geoffrey Wysdom asked the question again. His eyes were on her, very intent.

'I don't have much social life,' she said, quietly. 'I'm quite happy here in the evenings, reading. I go to a concert with a friend every few weeks, but I've never really felt the need for a social life.'

'Why?' Geoffrey Wysdom's voice was now so soft she found it difficult to hear him.

'What?'

'I said: why? – Why do you feel no need for a social life?'

She answered as well as she could his questions about her unexciting evenings, wondering of what interest they could possibly be to the viewers. Then suddenly someone said 'cut', and everything stopped.

The look of pain whipped magically off Geoffrey Wysdom's face, and he quickly lit another cigarette. He chatted on about his own social life, something about having to go to dinner with the Director General so many times it was almost becoming a bore. Virginia shifted her position slightly. It was very hot in the room, and she felt she was being dull.

When the cameras restarted, once again Geoffrey Wysdom assumed instant concern. He gave a small shrug of his grey flannel shoulders, and a little twisted smile, so that briefly his mouth showed again.

'Now some people might say, Virginia, that in this day and age it's a little strange for a girl of your age and your, er, looks, to be content with quite such a quiet life.' Pause.

'I suppose they might,' said Virginia.

'Now you are, I believe, still a virgin?' The uncertainty in his voice was curious, thought Virginia, considering the only reason he'd come here was her virginity.

'Yes, I am.'

Geoffrey Wysdom allowed a respectful silence to pass. Then he nodded two or three times, as if the gravity of the situation had only just come to him. Virginia, seeing no reason why she should be the one to break the silence, said nothing. Geoffrey Wysdom nodded again, but still the silence remained. At last he gave a kind of stifled sigh, and sympathetic pain shot through his eyes.

'And how does it *feel*, at your age, to be a virgin?'

Virginia felt a flicker of antipathy. She was brusque.

'It feels as it's always felt. As I have no idea what it must be like not to be a virgin, I obviously can't compare the situations. It's nothing I'm particularly proud of or, equally, worried about. When the time comes for me to be seduced, believe me, I shall give my fair share. But I don't spend my life craving for that time.'

She felt she had been quite as convincing about her lack of desire as he had been about his china, and smiled.

'I see.' A few more nods from Wysdom, slightly astonished this time. 'And have you any pictures in your mind about what it'll be like, when the time comes?'

Virginia quickly flicked through some of her well-remembered dreams.

'Oh yes. Absolutely. I'll be in a large field, breast-high in buttercups. It'll be summer. In the distance I'll see this beautiful young herdsman, very brown and thin, guiding a herd of cows. He'll leave them all and come over to me. Neither of us will speak, and he'll lash at the buttercups a bit with his stick, in a titillating sort of way, then he'll tear off my clothes and leap upon me, and the cows will be crashing about everywhere so we'll have to hurry before they get out on the road.' She stopped. Again there was silence. God, thought Geoffrey Wysdom, Jenny didn't tell me the girl was a case as well as a virgin: perhaps the two are synonymous. Still, it's lovely footage.

This time it was Virginia who helped Wysdom out of the silence.

'I mean,' she said, 'it would be an awful anticlimax, after thirty-one years, to end it all with an immemorable fumble in the back of a mini van, wouldn't it?'

'Yes. Yes, indeed.' Wysdom laughed slightly and touched his tie. The vivid pink reflected on to his fingers.

'Sorry, Geoff.' The cameraman was speaking. 'Could we go back over the cows bit again? We had a bit of trouble.'

37

Geoffrey Wysdom smiled bravely in the face of a break in the atmosphere.

'I'm so sorry,' he said to Virginia, 'technical troubles. Would you mind telling the story about the cowherd again? And add on the bit about the mini at the end, if you wouldn't mind, and then we'll just carry on.'

Virginia obediently repeated her dream, and even at the second telling Geoffrey Wysdom responded with a look of overpowering interest.

In the rest of the interview Virginia sensed that she disappointed Mr Wysdom. Was she happy in her virginity? Yes, she was. He looked a trifle downcast. Was there no private, promiscuous being within her trying to get out? No, there wasn't. Then how was it, in this day and age – he was a master of the softly spoken cliché – that she maintained her unusual state? Simply, that, believe it or not, Mr Wysdom (she refused to call him Geoffrey, though he kept calling her Virginia) the occasion for ending that state had never arisen. No one had ever asked her. A look of some disappointment crossed Wysdom's face, almost instantly replaced by one of sympathy. Perhaps, thought Virginia, he was expecting bloodcurdling stories of how she had fought off dozens of pursuers. Then she remembered the man in the Welsh graveyard, and decided it might cheer Wysdom up. But it was too late. Cut, said the cameraman, and Mrs Fly was cued in with coffee and all her best cups.

It was during this coffee break that Geoffrey Wysdom suggested, in a tortuous way, that Mr and Mrs Fly might like to join in what they in television called 'natural sync'. In other words, the Fly family would have a nice natural chat round the fire about virginity, while the cameras whirred, and none of them need worry because he, Geoffrey, would step in if anyone dried up. Mrs Fly was overcome. This unexpected bonus caused her to tremble again. She patted at her hair to disguise her excitement, and said in a shaky voice,

'I don't see why not, Ginny, do you? If it'll help the television people.'

'That's the spirit, that's the spirit,' encouraged Geoffrey Wysdom, his perceptive instincts telling him that the Flys were the very stuff that good natural sync was made of. Then, controlling his excitement at having won her over, he added in a serious voice,

'I think it would make a most valuable discussion, Mrs Fly.'

Mr Fly was less easily persuaded.

'It's not a subject I've ever discussed,' he said, plainly embarrassed. 'I have no views, really.'

'Come on, Ted. It's *different*, on television. People discuss all sorts of things,' his wife encouraged. Perhaps realising what it would cost him if he refused, Mr Fly lowered himself blushingly down on to the sofa, which put him closer physically to his wife than he had been for years, and agreed with an unhappy smile.

Geoffrey Wysdom then invited Virginia to pull up an armchair near her parents. She surprised him by declining.

'I'm afraid not,' she said. 'I've done my bit. If my parents like to discuss my virginity in front of the millions, they're welcome to do so. But nothing you can say will make me join them.' There was a hard edge to her voice. Geoffrey Wysdom quickly decided not to try to persuade her, and smilingly suggested she should merely listen. Maybe, when the time came, she would feel there was something she would like to say . . .

The whole performance started again. This time the director came out from his hiding place behind the armchair and sat in it instead, settling himself down, it seemed, with the happy confidence of one who is going to be well entertained for the next twenty minutes. Virginia sat beside him, noting the return of her mother's nervous rash, and the downward droop of her father's mouth, revealing that for him the whole business had gone too far, but who was he to fight the will of a great corporation?

'Mr Fly, as the father of a, er, pretty daughter who at thirty is still a virgin, can you tell me what you feel, *as* a father, about her well-preserved state in these days of free love and promiscuity?'

At the word 'pretty' Mr Fly's eyes briefly lit up. No one had ever described Virginia as pretty to him before, and unless he was a bigger sucker than he thought, this Mr Wysdom meant it. While pondering on these things Mr Fly missed the rest of the question, and so when it came to an end the room was filled with one of the now familiar silences.

'You see, Mr Fly, some people might say . . .' Geoffrey Wysdom started up again only to be interrupted by Mrs Fly, who could contain herself no longer.

'Let me say, speaking for my husband and I' (she nudged him in the ribs, at which point Mr Fly realised with dismay she had snatched away his answer and he had now lost his chance) '. . . let me say that Ted and I are proud of our daughter . . .'

It was with horror that Virginia then watched the interchange of ideas on the concept of virginity between her parents. She sensed that the crew, the director, Jenny and Geoffrey Wysdom were all inwardly patting themselves on the back. This, indeed, this ghastly spectacle of people knowing not what they say when the cameras are turned upon them, was for them most valuable natural sync. Geoffrey Wysdom only had to prod a little farther and Mrs Fly, drunk on the excitement of it all, would come out with the after-glow story. And that, naturally, would be far too good television to discard when it came to editing.

In spite of the heat in the room Virginia felt quite cold, and when the interview was over she went up to her room to put on a second cardigan.

The television people left with all the merry clamour they had come. Jenny gave Mrs Fly ten pounds cash for 'facilities' ('all the electricity we've used, and of course the coffee') and once again Mrs Fly was overcome almost to the point of speechlessness.

'My goodness, all the fun of it, and getting paid too,' she just managed to say. Geoffrey Wysdom repeated how valuable it had been to all of them, to him personally, and how *really* valuable it would be to the viewers. He shook hands with everyone, calling Mr and Mrs Fly Ted and Ruth by now, and left in a silver flash of his long car, designed once again to cause some wonder in the hearts of the neighbours.

When they had all gone Mrs Fly, with an effort to force herself back to reality, went to check on the lunch. Virginia paced the sitting-room marvelling at the renewed peace, the space, the quiet. On the one hand she despised herself for ever having agreed to do the interview. On the other hand, it left her full of a strange hope. Someone, somewhere, might be inspired by that smile.

She went to join her mother. Mrs Fly, apronless, was frying chips in a dream-like state. Suddenly, fat from the frying pan spat up on to the neck of her party dress, clotting a lump of the white cony fur. She looked down at it, for once uncaring.

'The price of fame,' was all she managed to say.

Chapter 3

On an evening late in January, in Ealing, Rita Thompson, widow, walked down the middle of a small street towards her house. She had a theory that by walking in the middle cars coming either way would be in no danger of not seeing her, and somehow it was safer than the shadows of the pavements.

Mrs Thompson, just turned fifty, was dressed as a fairy godmother. Not wanting to spoil her wings, which had taken two weeks hard work, cutting cardboard, pasting tinsel, spraying gold paint, and finally sewing a delicate harness to fit over her shoulders, she clutched her warm tweed coat under her chin, letting it fall over her front. This meant that her back, protected only by the magnificent wings and the thin, dyed parachute silk of her ball dress, was naked to the foggy air, and she shivered.

Mrs Thompson had been up at the old folk's club taking part in the pantomime. It had, she felt, been a success. And well it might have been. She and the girls – six other sporting, middle-aged ladies, had been rehearsing a condensed form of *Cinderella* for the past eight months. Whenever they all had a free evening, they had gathered in one or other of their houses, and put the thing together. It had been fun, mind. Oh, some of the laughs they'd had. Mrs Thompson's particular talent was thinking up the jokes: every joke in the script, she could honestly say, was her contribution. She had found them mostly in small print in the *Reader's Digest*, but some of the dirtier ones – they couldn't be *too* blue for the old folk –

she remembered from years of summer shows on various seaside piers.

They'd had their little differences, too, but that was to be expected, in eight months. There was the time when the casting was at a critical stage, and there had been a certain tension between Mrs Thompson and Mrs Wavell: both fancied themselves in the lead part. Mrs Wavell had it over Mrs Thompson in that she was a scraggy little thing, and a good ten years younger. But she did have a slight squint. Mrs Thompson had never imagined Cinderella with a squint, as she told her close friend Mrs Baxter, later: but she was too much of a gentlewoman to bring up that particular misgiving at the general meeting, and Mrs Wavell won the vote. Mrs Thompson forced herself to be a good sport about the whole thing. Apparently delighted at the idea of being the fairy godmother instead of Cinderella, she stood all the girls a round of sherries at The George that night to show there was no ill-feeling. The only thing she could not have borne would have been if everybody had instantly voted her to be one of the ugly sisters. But they didn't, because there were two obvious choices for these parts – Mrs Fields, who was no beauty but a great laugh, and Mrs Ryman, who knew herself to be the plainest woman in Ealing and said she didn't care.

Both the performances at the club had gone well, particularly the last one, to-night, when the actors had got over their nerves and were beginning to enjoy themselves. Mrs Thompson still thought, privately, more could have been made of Cinderella – for whom she'd written some lovely lines, in the days when she still felt a chance of playing the part herself. Mrs Wavell had a silly, simpering voice which didn't carry much beyond the first few rows of the church hall, and when she smiled at the prince her squinting eye – or did Mrs Thompson imagine it? –

seemed to lock itself more firmly against the side of her nose. But still, the main thing was, as Mrs Baxter had pointed out over the rock cakes afterwards, they'd given joy. The vicar himself had made a vote of thanks, and some of the old folk had tears in their eyes when the lights came on. Their pleasure gave Mrs Thompson a good feeling. 'Do as you would be done by' had always been her motto, and having enjoyed a splendid Christmas and New Year herself, it was rewarding to think the efforts of the last eight months had been worth it. She was pleased to feel she had been able to contribute to a scrap of happiness for those less fortunate than herself.

Mrs Thompson unlocked her front door – the plum paint was horribly chipped, but repainting it was one of the things she was never able to get round to doing – and let herself into the small, chilly front hall. She was met by a strong smell of potatoes, cabbage, onions and carrots – the vegetable stew she'd left in the oven, anticipating she'd be hungry. But now she was back, and the excitement was over, she didn't feel much like eating after all.

Judging by the silence in the house, the lodger, who had lived upstairs since Bill had died, was out. When he was in, he played his hi-fi almost continually, too loudly, a lot of pop stuff, nothing she liked very much. Sometimes she complained a little, and Jo (who was a perfect lodger in every other way) turned the music down a couple of decibels for a few days, then gradually it went back to its normal volume. But sometimes Mrs Thompson was quite grateful for the noise. To-night, for instance, she would have preferred it to the silence.

She went to her bedroom and began to grapple behind her back with the harness of her cardboard wings. When she had got them off she laid them on the double bed and contemplated them with some pride. They were a work of art, she thought: too good to be thrown away. She must find a place for them somewhere.

One of Mrs Thompson's economies, like sticking old bits of soap together and using envelopes twice, was to have no central heating in the bedroom. As a result, while contemplating the wings, arms crossed, she shivered. She was a large woman, but not ungainly. Plump thighs but good ankles; fleshy arms but delicate wrists; narrow hips but a solid stomach overshadowed by a hefty bosom. The blue parachute silk of her ball dress clung to her, revealing that in past years she must have had a good, sporting figure. Her neck was still well preserved, and though the skin of the face was beginning to sag, it was over good bones. She had wide apart, well-set eyes, sticky with blue shadow and thick false lashes, and a thin, wide mouth over which she had painted rather too bulbous red lips. She was, as her friend Mrs Baxter was always telling her, a marvel for fifty. Mrs Baxter even maintained that every-one would think the salt-and-pepper effect of Mrs Thompson's curly hair was entirely nature's work.

Now, alone in her bedroom, the evening still early, Mrs Thompson wondered what to do. She could of course go down to The George, as usual, but for some funny reason she didn't feel enthusiastic at the prospect this evening. In a strange way she wanted to keep on the blue silk dress for a few hours. It was only a tatty old thing, wartime material, run up in a few hours, but dressing up earlier on, and doing her face with especial care, had given Mrs Thompson the kind of kick she hadn't felt for a long time. It reminded her, she supposed, of her glamorous life thirty years ago – a time she hadn't, in fact, spoken of to anyone, including Bill or Mrs Baxter – but a glamorous time, in its way, all the same. In those days she had a nice little flat in Soho – two bedrooms, one for her Chinese maid, one for herself – and a room to receive in, which she kept strictly for friends. Her bedroom was papered in maroon flock wallpaper, and there were apple green satin sheets on the bed, sent by an anonymous admirer (she had her suspicions who he was). She had a whole small room full of clothes: beautiful fox furs, soft shiny velvet, satin and crêpe dresses, with shoes dyed to match each one. In those days, in her class of the profession, there was no vulgar business about dressing up warm to go out on the streets: she simply waited for the telephone to ring, sat back looking glamorous, and waited till her client arrived. She had her favourites, and they were good to her. Some brought her chocolates or flowers. They wafted in, in opera cloak and white kid gloves, smelling of their companion's expensive scent, and told her she was what they'd been waiting for the whole evening. She would offer them a tiny glass of Cointreau, and they would joke together, or talk quite seriously, some of them, or play a record, before getting down to business. Mrs Thompson received most of her education from her clients. From them she picked up smatterings of information about the opera, the theatre, politics, and stored it all up in her mind. Years later she would surprise Bill by coming up with some inside piece of information about Mr Chamberlain, for instance, and Bill would say:

'Where on earth did you gather that?' and she would always reply,

'I kept my ear to the ground, you know, dear.' He never guessed.

One of her clients – not exactly a gentleman, but he'd made a lot of money in shoes – sometimes took her to the theatre: she believed implicitly in mixing business with pleasure. On those occasions, Mrs Thompson felt, nobody would have taken her for anything but a lady of high birth. She dressed with impeccable taste: the blonde streaks in her pretty hair were as pale as moonbeams, and if her escort dared offer her an orchid on arrival, she would make some elegant excuse not to pin it on her coat or dress.

In four years at this job Rita made a lot of money. Even in those days she made her small economies – meat only once a week for the Chinese maid, only one gin and lime a day for herself – and she scrupulously saved for the vague future when she would be 'past it.' But long before she was past it she treated herself one year, after a particularly strenuous spring, to a ten day holiday in Monte Carlo. There, on the first night, she met Bill Thompson in the bar of her modest hotel. He was on business, something to do with the French railways – a tall, thick, jovial man, with a slight limp and a booming voice, fifteen years older than herself.

They fell in love in five minutes. Rita, who had been determined her rest would not turn into a busman's holiday, behaved decorously as a virgin. This fired Bill not only to greater passion, but to an honourable proposal of marriage within forty-eight hours.

Rita accepted, cut her holiday short, and raced back to England. There, she quickly sold her flat, her beautiful clothes, and sacked the Chinese maid. Equally swiftly she took a small, gloomy room in the Bayswater Road and bought herself some plain, sensible skirts and jerseys. By the time Bill arrived back in London he found her happily settled in what he imagined had been her home for years, and which he was determined to release her from as soon as possible. The only reminder Rita had kept of the past were a few trinkets – silver ashtrays and porcelain figures – which some of her clients had given her on special occasions. These she put behind glass on lighted shelves, and said she had inherited them from her family. Bill, for his part, was pleased to think his wife had the kind of family who left her nice things.

They moved to the flat in Ealing (now the lodger's flat) and bought the freehold of the whole house ten years later. Rita never managed to have any children. They decided at one time to adopt some, but then the war came, and when it was over they abandoned the idea. Nevertheless they were, as Mrs Baxter often pointed out, an ideal couple: a rarity in these days of easy come, easy go, in marriage, and they remained loving to the last, which was in 1965, when Bill died of lung cancer.

Since then Rita, who wasn't one to let things get her down, however traumatic, had taken a hold on herself, as she called it. She had started helping out at the old people's club not long after Bill died, and regularly visited some of the members who were confined to their homes, cheering them with her gay laugh and gossipy stories. She had also taken a course in typing and did occasional work for a retired general in Knightsbridge, whose failing sight meant he overlooked most of her mistakes. Apart from that, she knitted very complicated jerseys, some of which she sold to an elderly boutique off Oxford Street: and she had her acquaintances and her one good friend, Mrs Baxter. Alternate Tuesdays she and Mrs Baxter visited each other's houses for a prolonged high tea, followed by a drink in The George, and sometimes went to a musical or a film. But in spite of the busyness of her life – and never for one moment would Mrs Thompson let anyone think it was not overflowing with activity – there were still many unfilled gaps during the day, and sometimes the evenings were long. On those occasions familiar worries filled her mind, haunting her. She tried to suppress them, but never could succeed.

As she pulled one of her own brightly knitted jerseys over her head, down over the shiny parachute silk dress, once again some of these thoughts shot aggressively into

her head, so that she clapped her hand over her mouth
and groaned out loud. Should she or shouldn't she have
told Bill? Should she have let him go to the grave deceived,
and happy? Or should she have spoiled his illusions, and
possibly wrecked their marriage? All these questions,
asked a million times in the last thirty years, she could
never answer, never put to anyone else: only wonder to
herself. It was too late, anyway, to do anything about
it. Bill could never know now. There was no way of
relief.

With a sigh of impatience at herself Rita made her way
to the kitchen. She still walked with a certain allure –
small strides, bottom slightly shaking. 'Sexy,' Bill used to
call her, sometimes, on Saturday nights. 'Wouldn't be safe
to let you anywhere without me.'

The kitchen was a small balloon of warmth – a faded,
chipped room, but cosy. It had an armchair, a budgerigar,
and the television on the dresser. Rita spent most of her
time here these days. She could never like the front room
with its three-piece suite and wedding pictures and brass
coal scuttle. She only used it for parties, and she didn't
have many of those, now.

Bending down over the oven, she took out her vegetable
stew, a little brown round the edges, but bubbling and
smelling good. She laid herself a place at the table –
spoon, fork and knitted table mat – because she liked to
keep up her standards, alone or not. Then, on a sudden
whim, she went to one of the cupboards and took out a
half-bottle of whisky. Normally, she never drank at home.
But to-night she felt she needed it.

She drank half the glass and immediately felt better,
instantly warmer. Her lost appetite came back, and she
dug hungrily into the stew.

For a while the quiet in the room was only interrupted
by the gentle supping noises she made, sucking up the

gravy. But then it began to rain, and she could hear the icy tinkle of drops hitting the window pane, and the sad yowl of the lodger's cat outside.

Oh, Ethelberta, she thought. I must let her in. He's not fit to have an animal, Jo. She didn't really mean this: Jo was all over his cat, gave him every consideration. It was just that the words 'he's not fit to have an animal, Jo,' went through her head, noisy as the rain, unordered.

She went to the back door and opened it. The cat streaked in on a squall of wind and a blast of rain, its black coat wetly matted and dull.

'Go on Ethelberta, off with you! What were you doing out there?' Ethelberta needed no encouragement to vanish. She flashed across the linoleum floor, out of the other door, and up the stairs.

Left to herself again, Rita sat down at the table once more, finished off the stew, conscious that she was making a pig of herself and would never get thin this way, then pushed back her empty plate. She finished the whisky, and glanced above her at the lightshade. It was a pretty gingham thing, like Miss Muffet's bonnet. She'd made it years ago, and now it was burnt on one side, discoloured and limp. She'd been meaning to make a new one for ages. All of a sudden, staring up at it, tears began to run thickly down her cheeks. She gave a great sniff, and patted her eyes with her paper napkin, which came away from them streaked with blue and black.

'What on earth's the matter now, you silly old fool?' she asked herself, out loud. 'This is no way to carry on.' And then, half despising herself, she went to the television and turned it on.

It was that man – what was his name? – Geoffrey Wysdom. She recognised the voice before the picture came on. Well, he would do her good, no doubt. He always talked to people a good deal worse off than her, at any rate, and if he did so to-night that would make her count her blessings. She sniffed, and watched.

There was a close up on the screen of a girl with a thin, pale face and round dark eyes. She had a quiet but firm voice, and seemed not to be looking at Geoffrey Wysdom, but at something beyond.

'I'll be in a large field, breast-high in buttercups,' she was saying. 'It'll be summer. In the distance I'll see this beautiful young herdsman, very brown and thin, guiding a herd of cows. He'll leave them all and come over to me. Neither of us will speak, and he'll lash at the buttercups a bit with his stick, in a titillating sort of way . . .' A smile flickered round her mouth, tearing at Mrs Thompson's heart. Entranced, she rested her head in her hands, and watched the rest of the programme without sniffing once. When it was over, she cried again, but this time with elation.

Inspiration had come to her. It sometimes did, at opportune moments, and this was one of them. There she was, self-pitying old fool, she told herself, with a comparatively good life on her hands. How could she indulge in the self-pity of this evening, when out there in Surrey there was this tragic young girl, still a virgin at thirty-one, who needed help, and friends, and men. It wasn't only the old who were indigent. Well, she, Rita Thompson, woman of the world, would stretch out a hand to Virginia Fly, virgin. Here was a chance for them both.

Flushed, partly by the thought of her new project, and partly by the whisky, Mrs Thompson took out her writing pad. She would have to think carefully. It would be no easy matter, this letter. Writing scripts for pantomimes was a piece of cake in comparison. She took up her pen.

Dear Miss Virginia Fly, she began.

Mrs Fly took the opportunity of the television programme

to ask in a considerable bunch of neighbours. She began preparing for her party several days before necessary, and ended up with far too many plates of small biscuits with smaller coloured things on top of them. Mr Fly had been prevailed upon to buy a lot of cheap red wine which Mrs Fly warmed and spiced, to welcome her friends as they came in from the coldness of the night.

Virginia disapproved of the whole idea of the party. Left on her own, she wouldn't have watched the programme at all. In retrospect the event was obnoxious to her, and she regretted ever having agreed to do it. But having made her mistake there was nothing she could do but brave the consequences. She only agreed to attend the party because when she had suggested going out her mother became so hurt, indignant and offended that facing the party seemed more bearable than putting up with days of martyrdom.

'For heaven's sake, Ginny,' said Mrs Fly, peevishly, 'we'll be the stars of the evening. It'll be our night. It's not every day anyone from Acacia Avenue is on television.'

And the people of Acacia Avenue did, in fact, treat Virginia as a star. A couple of them brought autograph books. A middle-aged married man, who had never before given her so much as a glance, nudged her hard in the ribs and inquired what was the price of fame? When the mulled wine came in they all drank her health and future success on the box, as they called it. Virginia hated every moment of the proceedings. It also began to occur to her that her mother had not told anybody what the programme was about. She took her chance to ask. Mrs Fly, her normal colour already heightened by her sense of occasion, blushed a deeper salmon.

'Well, I told them it was a *serious* programme, dear. Not one of those stupid quiz games.'

'But what did you tell them it was about?'

'Oh, I don't know. People and their problems, I think I said. They'd all heard of Geoffrey Wysdom, of course. They know the kind of programme he does.'

'But this particular programme isn't about problems. It's about various attitudes of mind to different ways of life before marriage.'

'Well, I don't think I said that, exactly. I said it was something to do with not getting married very young, I think. Now, don't bother me, dear. You can see I've got things to do. Pass round the Twiglets, would you?'

Virginia turned away, sickened. She drank two glasses of wine very fast to cloud her senses. Then, with relief, she found that the humour of the situation began to appeal to her. The neighbours imagined they were here for a good party. They were all smiles, all asking obvious questions about was it frightening, and how did it feel to be famous? They imagined she was going to answer a few questions about being a spinster, or something. Very interesting. Virginia wondered how their countenances would have changed in an hour's time. What appropriate remarks they could find to make *then*.

The programme began. A girl who had just had a back-street abortion was interviewed, followed by a girl whose fiancé had managed to hold out till a few weeks before the wedding, then raped her and left her. She was in tears throughout the interview.

'A very *serious* programme, Ruth,' said one of the neighbours, who felt happier watching Tom Jones.

'Very serious,' admitted Mrs Fly, 'but very worthwhile.'

Virginia came on to the screen. Mrs Fly gave a muted groan of ecstasy and motherly pride.

'What a good likeness,' she said. 'Ted, isn't it?'

Mr Fly grunted something in reply. The rest of the audience remained in dumbfounded silence.

Virginia watched the interview up to the point when Geoffrey Wysdom asked her how it felt to be a virgin in this day and age? She watched her small, calculated smile before she answered that question, then got up to leave the room.

'Where are you going?' hissed Mrs Fly, anxious that no one should miss the moment when she herself would appear on the screen.

'Out.'

'But you can't. Not at this time of night. Besides, people will *know* you, now.'

Ignoring this remark, Virginia closed the door on the television spectacular, knowing her mother would not follow her at so crucial a moment. She put on her coat, went outside, and began to walk down the deserted Acacia Avenue. It was very cold, a little frosty. But her only concern was to walk until the programme was over, the neighbours had stopped twittering about her virginity, and had gone home.

By now she could no longer think whether she had done right or wrong, had made a fool of herself or a heroine. The only thing she knew positively was that her smile had been endearing, and there was a fair chance of it captivating someone, somewhere.

And if it didn't, well, never mind. It was only a couple of days till Charlie arrived. Only a couple of days until her whole life changed.

Professor Hans Meiselheim's flat was the ground floor of a Georgian house in Hampstead. He had lived in it for twenty years, and as the rent had only gone up minimally in that time and the landlady, who lived upstairs, was a particularly agreeable and uninterfering woman, he had no thoughts of ever leaving it.

It consisted of a small bedroom, bathroom and kitchen, and a very large, high-ceilinged sitting-room whose deep windows overlooked the Heath. It was a comfortable, cluttered room: Regency striped wallpaper in two shades of red on the walls, dull maroon velvet curtains whose edges were faded by the sun to the colour of vin rosé; a few sagging sofas and chairs, books and records piled everywhere, a wood fire, and, among a collection of cacti on the mantelpiece, a solitary photograph of a fair-haired woman and young child walking in an Alpine landscape. This was Christabel, his wife, and Gretta, his daughter, killed together in an air crash twenty years ago.

On the evening of Virginia's television programme the professor, as usual, was at his desk making notes for a lecture he was to give the next day. The desk was a shadowy litter of papers that had accumulated over the years, and the professor's notebook itself was scarcely lit by the weak bulb under a thick old parchment lampshade. The professor was bent low over his notes, conscious of the scratching of his pen, the thud of rain on the window, and the occasional spitting of the fire.

He came at last to the end of his work and gave a deep, audible sigh. Pushing himself back from his desk he stood up, stretched, scratched under each arm, and went to stretch out his hands in front of the fire. The white joints of his knuckles cracked as he moved each finger.

It was now time for his customary whisky and soda, and had he followed the normal pattern of his evenings, he would then have gone to the small kitchen, cut himself a hunk of cold meat from Sunday's joint, taken a baked potato out of the oven, added pickles and a lump of cheese to the plate, and had his supper in front of the fire. But this evening he felt an unaccountable restlessness. Neither cold lamb nor Cheddar cheese appealed to him. What he needed, he felt, was a cigar and some Tchaikovsky. He put on a record, lit himself a cigar, poured a neat whisky, and returned to the mantelpiece.

There, he realised, he had done a foolish thing. Tchaikovsky and a strong drink, when faced with the picture of Christabel, could induce in him melancholy thoughts. He had often thought of throwing the picture away. In fact he had often gone so far as to throw it away, untorn, and then retrieved it next day from the wastepaper basket. He had burned everything else many years ago – all Christabel's letters in her schoolgirl hand, her curl of white-blonde hair, her diaries, her pressed flowers, all the sheet-music he had marked for her during the years he was her tutor. But the photograph had survived twenty years of his indecision, and he knew he would never be able to part with it now, foolish though it may be to keep it.

He had taken it only six months before Christabel and Gretta died. It was a Sunday afternoon, in the mountains near Salzburg. Christabel's face was flushed from a morning of sun and exercise, and Gretta kept interrupting the walk to roll down through the long emerald grass, so that Hans had to run after her and climb back up the mountainside with her on his shoulders. They had had a picnic lunch of salami and goat's cheese and wine, and caught the bus back to Salzburg – in those days they were much too poor to own a car – at dusk.

Six months later Hans, who had struggled for five years to live on the meagre earnings from his piano teaching, and occasional sales of his compositions, learned he had won a competition set in London for writing an orchestral suite. He was invited over to conduct a public performance of his work. With his winnings he bought air tickets for his wife and daughter so that they should be with him on the great night. They flew over. Christabel shared his triumph. Well-known musicians shook him by the hand, and complimented Christabel on her beauty. With one accord the critics claimed him to be a great potential talent. As a result, he was offered various jobs in England, all of which seemed preferable to his old life in Salzburg. It was necessary for him to stay on in London for a few days to sort things out. But he couldn't afford for Christabel and Gretta to stay with him. He took them to the airport, where they were photographed kissing each other good-bye – a remarkably handsome young couple, as the papers said, and on the way back the aeroplane crashed. All aboard dead.

Hans turned down all the offers of jobs, but stayed in London. He never returned to Salzburg, and wrote no more music.

His fingers now played on his thigh, following the notes of the piano concerto that sang through the room, and he hummed a little, slightly out of tune.

This is ridiculous, he thought, the words loud in his head as the music. Ridiculous. I will ask Mrs Beveridge to join me in a drink. That will dispel the depression.

At the thought of a drink with his landlady in her small, rickety kitchen with its dripping tap and snoring poodle, the frown disappeared from the professor's brow, and he poured a second drink as strong as his own.

Mrs Beveridge was sitting at her kitchen table filling in her pools coupons. The room smelt of curry.

'Oh, hallo, professor. How's things?' She smiled nicely at him and stretched out her hand for the drink. 'Here's to. Been to any good concerts, lately?' She had asked him precisely the same question only yesterday morning, when they had met at the front door collecting the papers: but it was her custom always to start conversations with him like that. It was the one subject that got him going.

That and Austria, and she couldn't for the life of her think what to ask about Austria just at this very moment.

'No. Not for one month, two months I think it is now.' Not since he and Virginia had been to the terrible Mozart woman.

'Well, I expect it's the wrong time of year.'

The professor sat himself opposite Mrs Beveridge at the kitchen table.

'Funnily enough,' Mrs Beveridge was saying, 'I was just going to take myself next door to watch Geoffrey Wysdom's programme. You know. Like to join me?'

'That would be a pleasure.' On many occasions he had come up to Mrs Beveridge to watch a televised concert and she had sat quietly by him supplying cups of tea. It would only be the polite and kind thing to do to join her in her kind of programme.

'Soon as we've finished the hard stuff I can put on the kettle.'

She was bustling about, moving the small electric fire from the kitchen to her uncomfortable sitting-room with its upright sofa and musty smell of old material. They sat side by side in the dark watching the television. The professor felt a small flicker of indigestion rise in his chest. He heard, but did not take in, the mumblings of the interviews. His eyelids lowered gently over his eyes.

Then Virginia came on to the screen. Surely it was Virginia? He made no movement, just waited for her voice. Yes, it was her. Virginia Fly. The man with the hushed voice said so. Virginia Fly, he said. And then she smiled, a small, touching, lost smile. A stab of pain went through the professor's chest.

'My God.' He clapped his hand to his head.

'What is it, dear?' Mrs Beveridge shuffled round in the dark to see his face. Lit only by the picture on the screen, she could see that it was twisted with pain.

'That is a friend of mine,' he said. 'A friend of mine

'Oh? How interesting. I expect they found her, you know, when they went out into the street with a camera.'

'No. It's nothing like that,' he heard himself snap. For the first time in twenty years Mrs Beveridge irritated him.

They both listened in silence to the interview. Then the professor, asking Mrs Beveridge to excuse him, quickly left the room.

He hurried back to his own flat, turned on just one dim light, and sat down at the piano. He played a few notes, and then his hands slid into his lap.

'My child,' he said out loud. 'My child, what have you done?'

He stood up and went to the desk. He felt a little unsteady. The whisky must have been stronger than usual. He fiddled with a piece of clean writing paper and his pen. Then the solution came to him. He believed in the remedial values of positive action. He picked up his pen and concentrated on the steadiness of his hand.

My Dear Virginia, he wrote, *To-night I listened to you on the television, and I saw you smile . . .*

Chapter 4

Charles Whitmore Oakhampton Jr. arrived at London Airport on a Friday. It was a nasty February afternoon, grey, with a slanting bitter wind that whipped his ears as he descended the steps to the tarmac. He thought, simply, gee: what a beginning. Perhaps he should have waited for the spring after all. But he had been postponing the trip for so many years. He was glad at last to have taken the bull by the horns, and as his father had told him, if you could love England in February, you could love it any time.

Virginia had written him she would not be able to meet him because of school. She was coming up later, in the evening. They were to have dinner together, not far from the hotel, and see the cabaret. She had booked herself a room in his hotel and would stay in London for the weekend to show him the sights.

On the bus, on the way into London, Charlie took from his wallet a grubby little list on which he had doodled and made amendments to pass the time on the aeroplane. *Stratford*, it said. *Windsor, Tower, British Museum, Zoo, Madame Tussauds, Tiberio Restaurant, football match (Chelsea), Canterbury, Vera Lynch.* Canterbury he intended to go to because his maternal grandmother had come from there, somewhere called New Street – nine children brought up in a three-roomed house, his mother had said. He'd believe it when he saw it. After New Street, if there was time, he'd take a look at the cathedral. Vera Lynch was the name of a girl in a china shop in Regent Street with whom he'd been corresponding, about china, for the last five months, having seen an advertisement in *The New Yorker*.

Charlie was tired. But not too tired to appreciate his first glimpse of Piccadilly Circus, tatty in the drizzle, choked with shining wet traffic and a thousand umbrellas. Gee, he thought again.

He checked into his hotel, helping himself to a pile of Travel in Britain and Welcome to Britain brochures while he waited. Then he went up to his room, opened his dent-resistant suitcase (because his mother had taught him that clothes, like humans, need air after a journey), lay on the bed without taking off the slippery cover, and slept.

When he woke, three hours later, he had a bad taste in his mouth, and his head felt heavy. Outside he could hear the drone of traffic. He rang for a Coke and bourbon. It appeared twenty-five minutes later, with no ice. But rather than complain, he drank it warm. Slowly, he felt better.

He unpacked, showered, changed. He slicked on hair grease, ran an orange stick round his nails, and slapped his neck with after-shave called *Beast*. He'd had it sent, mail order, from Kentucky. Then he sat in the one armchair reading his trayelogues, waiting.

At precisely eight o'clock, the bell rang. Charlie counted three to himself, out loud, then strode slowly across the room to the door. Opened it. Before him stood a small, pale, thin girl with scraped-back coppery hair and huge blurry eyes. She stood huddled in the fur collar of her coat as if the blue carpeted corridor was a vast waste, and she was deserted, with no hope of ever seeing human habitation again.

'Virginia Fly!' He rolled the R.

'Charlie Oakhampton!' A narrow smile widened the edges of her mouth, forcing a play of light and shade round her cheeks and eyes. Charlie found himself walking backwards into the room. Virginia followed him, shutting the door behind her as she went, feeling for the handle.

'Why, Virginia Fly, after all these years.' Somewhere near the bed he squeezed her shoulders, feeling the bones.

'I know. Isn't it extraordinary?' She looked up at him. 'You're quite like your photograph. I mean, I would have known you.'

'You would? Well.' Pause. 'Well. How about that?' They looked at each other again. 'This calls for a celebration. How about a drink? D'you like champagne? Let's go down to the bar. There's plenty of time before the cabaret. We can go on over in a cab.'

'We could walk, in fact,' said Virginia. 'It's only a few yards.'

'We'll walk, then. We'll walk. I could do with stretching my legs after that journey, I can tell you.'

'Are you sure you're not too tired?' Virginia was vaguely hesitant.

'Good heavens, no, Virginia. Good heavens, no. I'm on top of the world, I'm telling you. After all these years, here I am in London.'

In the lift he sensed that Virginia was a little tremulous, not quite relaxed, in spite of the twelve years of letters between them. A couple of glasses would do the trick, he thought. A couple of glasses.

Virginia slipped off her coat in the bar, to reveal a plain brown dress in jersey stuff, high to the neck, with a small pearl brooch on one shoulder. Charlie stared, fascinated. He could see her heart beating. Quickly he ordered champagne. When it came he held up his glass and drank to her.

'Here's to the end of our course in correspondence, and on to something more tangible.' A shudder went down Virginia's spine. Charlie smiled at her, friendly. She noticed his bottom teeth were thinly edged with black, as if each one was in an individual frame. Strange. She thought American dentists were meant to be the best in the world.

They ate salted nuts. Charlie kept on smiling.

'Well, Virginia Fly, one thing I must say: you're the greatest little letter writer in the world. The greatest. I've never had such letters. I looked forward to them, you know. For twelve years I've looked forward to your letters. That's quite something.'

Virginia couldn't, in all honesty, return the compliment in its entirety. He was not an imaginative letter writer, but it was true she looked forward to his letters all the same. She said so.

'Why, that's really nice of you, Virginia.' He laid one of his huge hands on her wrist, and spoke very low. 'Say, wouldn't it have been awful if we'd been disappointed in each other? If we'd found each other ugly and boring?' He was so close to her she could smell strong toothpaste on his breath and a whiff of *Beast* coming from his thick neck. She quivered again – a familiar sensation. It was how she felt when approached by the dark-moustached man of her dreams. But she couldn't think of anything to say. So Charlie went on:

'You know, I guess there's practically nothing about you I don't know – except of course, how you feel, what you're like to touch – ' He gave a great bellowing laugh. Other nearby drinkers looked up. Virginia blushed, spluttered over her champagne and raised her second hand to her glass to steady it, forcing Charlie to leave go of her wrist. 'There, now. Don't say I've upset you? It was only a joke.' Virginia smiled slightly. 'No, but you know what I mean. I could walk into any part of your house and feel I'd been there a thousand times before – the way you describe it. I know what your bit of garden looks like in spring, summer, autumn and winter. I know all about your schoolroom – cold in the mornings, isn't it,

63

didn't you say? I'd recognise the professor in any crowd –
you describe it all so beautifully. I'd do anything to have
a gift like that, myself.'

'I have a very dull life, really,' said Virginia. 'Nothing
ever happens. I always think it must make dull letters. So
perhaps I colour it a bit, make it sound more interesting
than it really is.'

They chattered on in a monochrome sort of way about
their letters. Three glasses of champagne made everything skid about a little in Virginia's vision, pleasantly.
She found she could talk to Charlie without thinking and,
equally, listen to him without thinking. Behind the drum
of the words small pictures, like a miniature light-show,
worked in her mind: Charlie across the breakfast table
in a few years' time, face more creased, but arms still
muscular under his tee shirt; Charlie in gym shoes,
bouncing on the balls of his feet, kicking a ball to one of
their sons; Charlie, executive, picking her up from the
supermarket in a Cadillac . . . All the neat confines of an
American suburban life. She would like that. She would
be a good wife to Charlie. She had never imagined anything else. No other possibility had ever presented itself.

They walked to the restaurant. It was still drizzling and
cold. Virginia took Charlie's arm and he took her hand.
He inhaled great puffs of air, letting them out with a lot
of noise. They rose in visible clouds of smoke into the
multi-coloured rain.

'It's polluted air,' apologised Virginia. To-night, Piccadilly Circus looked totally unfamiliar.

In thirty years, she had never been to a place remotely
like the restaurant they now entered. It appeared to her
in a mosaic of shaded lights and sparkling bosoms and
high piles of lacquered curls. They seemed to be the
youngest couple there, and it occurred to Virginia that
compared with the scintillating average she must appear

very drab. She was grateful to the dim lighting: perhaps no one would notice.

They sat at a tiny table at the edge of a galleried tier, looking down on more eaters and an elaborate stage. The table was so small Virginia had to put her bag on the ground, and it was impossible for her knees not to touch Charlie's underneath it.

'This is what I call close,' said Charlie. 'Great.'

He ordered himself a large Martini – Virginia refused another drink – and dinner. It was while Virginia found herself hesitating between the fillet of steak and the fried scampi it occurred to her that up to now she had been a little dull. She felt the first uneasy sensations of panic within her. Several more hours of the evening to go, and so far she had done nothing to be attractive. She must liven up.

'You must come home one day,' she said, in a voice that was so bright it surprised even her. 'Mother and Father have been looking forward to meeting you for years. Mother says your photograph is so – good looking.' She smiled shyly.

'Why, that's nice of her. I'd love to come on down. I tell you what. This weekend I thought we'd put by for sight-seeing, the Tower and all that. Monday through Friday next week I have a little business to attend to – I have to go to Manchester, I think it is, then I return here Saturday. Perhaps I could come on down then, and go from your house to the airport Sunday next?'

'On Sunday?'

'Yeah. Why?'

'I thought – I thought you were staying, well, almost indefinitely.'

'Oh no, honey. I can't do that, now, can I? There's work to be done.'

Virginia bit her lip. She tried to recall her mistake. She

65

was positive he'd said he'd be over for some weeks, no definite date to go home . . . How, if he was leaving in a week, could all the arrangements be made in time? Well, no doubt he had some plan.

'I suppose there is. You must be very busy.'

'Expansion, you know. We're expanding all the time. I have to be away from home more and more. Contact making from coast to coast.'

'Your mother must miss you.' She remembered how in his letters he wrote a lot about his mother. He was particularly fond of her and actively missed her when they were apart. Charlie nodded but didn't reply. A little desperately Virginia tried to think what else Charlie wrote about. Strangely, it all seemed to have gone from her mind.

'Your baseball – do you still play every weekend?'

'Not as much as I used to. But yes, I do play most Saturday afternoons. Yeah.' He was drinking his third large Martini.

Dinner came, small helpings of rather tasteless food served swiftly without elegance. They ate it in almost complete silence. Then the noisy cabaret, a lot of sparkling dancers, followed by a weedy comedian in a dazzling dinner jacket. Charlie didn't smile because he didn't understand the jokes. Virginia didn't smile because she had a headache.

When Charlie asked Virginia to dance she followed him on to the floor wondering why the glamour, the great burst of glamour that had struck her when they came into the place, had evaporated. Down here on the floor the other customers, for all their false-hair and eyelashes and smiles and jewels, looked old and shabby, and the men were uniformly ugly. They hadn't even got nice faces. She felt fleetingly proud of Charlie.

He danced quite well, but his hands were sweaty. He

pushed his mouth into her hair and his loins against her stomach. She felt something in her throat begin to pulsate, so that it was hard to swallow and she forgot her headache.

'You're great, baby,' he whispered, and clutched her tighter as the band wafted into a funeral version of "Blue Moon."

Back at the hotel, as Virginia's room was on the top floor and Charlie's on the first, he suggested it would be more practical to stop off at his room for a nightcap. Virginia agreed. Coffee, she needed.

The room, lit only by the bedside light, looked slightly less offensive than it had done earlier. The dim light deadened somewhat the glare of the satinette curtains and the mock wood wardrobes. It was stiflingly hot.

Virginia took off her coat and sat in the only armchair. Charlie, too, took off his jacket and shoes and heaved himself on to the high, turned-down bed. He folded his hands awkwardly, like a man unused to prayer, and contemplated Virginia.

'Well, honey,' he said, 'the night is young.'

Virginia smiled. She wondered how long she should stay before he would think she wanted to be seduced, and she wondered how and when he would bring up the subject of their future.

The waiter arrived with coffee and bourbon. Charlie tipped him but didn't say thank you. Virginia imagined he must be preoccupied.

She took her coffee back to the armchair. Charlie remained on the bed.

'Tell me about your life,' he said.

'You know all about my life.'

'I only know what you've written me. That can't be all. There must be a lot you've left out.'

'No, I don't think so. It's just, as I said, I lead a very

quiet life.' Charlie looked at her with a quizzical smile, his lips wet from the drink.

'You've never mentioned any lovers.'

'Lovers?' Virginia laughed. 'I've never had any lovers. If you'd arrived a week earlier you could have seen me on a television programme explaining what it felt like to be a thirty-one-year-old virgin.'

'Really? No joking?'

'No joking.'

Charlie was silent for a moment. Then he said: 'You know something? I think I believe you.'

'Well, it's true.'

'I've never met *any* kind of a virgin before, as far as I recall, let alone a thirty-one-year-old one. That's quite something.' Virginia felt his tone was admiring.

'These days,' she said, 'people go on about virgins as if they were museum pieces. We're perfectly ordinary human beings, you know, but we just haven't come across the chance. Chance, in respectable suburbia, isn't as plentiful as the women's magazines make out.'

'You sound quite defiant.'

'I'm not really defiant. I'm used to being a curiosity.'

Charlie loosened his tie and undid the top button of his shirt.

'Hey, what about some bourbon?'

'I've never tasted it. I don't think I'd like it.'

'Have a try.' He filled the second glass but didn't move from the bed. 'It's good stuff. Come on.'

Virginia went over to him. He gave her the glass. She took a sip and made a face. Charlie laughed.

'Have another try. It needs a little perseverance.' In persevering himself, Virginia noticed, he had already drunk almost half the bottle.

This time, while she took another sip, he put his hand round her bottom and patted it. She stood, transfixed, the glass poised at her mouth, the colour rushing to her face. Unable to move she felt his hand creep under the back of her skirt and scratch her thigh.

'I don't like it,' she said, finally.

'What, the bourbon?' Again Charlie laughed, rather swimmily, wrinkling up his nose and showing a lot of brownish gum. Virginia put her glass back on the tray. Charlie did likewise. Then he took both her wrists.

'Well, beautiful, thirty-one years is like a long time.'

Virginia felt immensely hot, her clothes were too tight and there was a constriction in her throat. Now, she knew, was the time to leave.

'Yes,' she heard herself saying, 'it's a long time, but as I said, there's never really been the opportunity – '

'What the hell do you think I am if not the opportunity?' Charlie had raised his voice and there were bubbles in the corner of his mouth. Before Virginia could answer he had dragged her down to him, was holding on to her head by the hair, and kissing her greedily.

'Oh, no, Charlie. Please.' Virginia tried to drag herself away from him. She half wanted not to resist him, but he was too rough, too fast. 'I must go to bed.'

'Indeed you must, Virginia Fly. Indeed you must.' He suddenly pushed her away from him but still kept hold of her wrists. His hair, crew-cut, was standing straight up. Virginia longed to smooth it down. 'Christ, what a girl.' He spoke more gently. Then he let go of one of her wrists, and ran his hand down from her shoulder over her breast, and finally latched on to her waist. 'Come on, honey. Don't wait any more. I'll be careful of you.'

Virginia felt tears pricking her eyes. She didn't say anything, but made to back away from Charlie. He let go of her.

'Do you really want to go?'

A kind of roulette wheel spun in her head, marked with

the words Yes and No. At which word would the spinning wheel stop?

'No,' she said.

'Of course you don't.' His words were a little thick, smug. His smile knowing. He didn't do anything about his hair. 'Let's get into bed, then.'

He ripped off his shirt very fast, unzipped his trousers and threw them on to the floor. Then he lay back on the bed again in tight, aerated underpants and duck-egg blue angora socks. Virginia remained motionless, looking at his body. He was muscular, pale, big. His stomach rolled over the elastic of his pants. His legs were matted with sandy hair.

'Come on. I'll help you,' he said. Virginia went over to him as if in a trance, turned round and let him unzip her dress. Letting it fall to the ground, she stepped out with her back still to him. She felt his hands running over her shoulder blades and swooping towards the fastening of her bra.

'No!' She gasped.

'I'll do it.' He had already undone it and was slipping the straps over her shoulders. 'Oh, Charlie!' She felt ludicrous.

'Turn round, honey. You can't keep your back to me all night.' He sounded a little impatient.

Putting her hands over her breasts, Virginia turned round slowly.

'That's my girl.'

Virginia closed her eyes. *God, please don't let him do it with his socks on*, she prayed. With her eyes still closed she pulled off her tights and pants. Charlie was laughing.

'What's the matter?'

'You're doing that thing like when one was a child: shut your own eyes and you think no one else can see you. I can see you all right. You've a great little body.'

Virginia opened her eyes. Charlie was licking his lips and sniffing. His underpants stirred. His eyes were all over her body. She stepped back again.

'Well, let's get on with it.' He stood up, towering over her, and took off the pants, his eyes still on her. She felt the blood surging round her face. Never in her life had she been so burning hot.

Charlie put out his hands towards her. Reluctantly, Virginia uncovered her breasts again and gave him her hands. She let her eyes rove over his face, his shoulders, his chest. But they would go no lower. She looked back at his face.

'Come on. You've got to look at it some time.' He seemed to be mocking, his promised gentleness forgotten.

Suddenly she snatched her hands away from him, ran over to the armchair, and huddled in its seat, her arms round her folded legs. She still hadn't been able to bring herself to look lower than his navel.

'Now come on honey, give me a chance. I'm too old to run around rooms.'

Virginia forced herself to glance at him. He stood half in a patch of light from the lamp: legs apart, hands on hips, hair still ridiculously askew, a sneering smile, the protruding stomach, a huge purple erection poised to snap her virginity for ever, and the blue angora socks.

'What's the matter?' He put his head on one side, wrinkled up his nose and gave a loud burp. 'Pardon me'.

'Nothing really. It's just that you're so huge.' Virginia cast down her eyes.

'Sure, I'm huge. What did you expect? I'm a tall man. Things come in proportion.'

He was beginning to walk towards her, slowly. She noticed that one of his socks had slipped down a little, revealing a smooth white rim of leg where the hairs stopped. He stood before her, legs astride again, the whole

71

of his desirous apparatus perilously close to her face, the vast cock gently bobbing up and down like a clumsy mobile. Virginia hastily scrambled to a standing position on the chair: there was no room for her to stand on the floor in front of it without Charlie touching her.

'Please,' she whispered, 'just one thing. Could you take off your socks?'

Charlie looked surprised.

'Sure, honey, anything to oblige.' Without moving his position from the chair he raised each knee in turn, pulled off each sock, and let them fall on the floor. There they settled into two creamy blue blobs on the hideous checked carpet. 'Tell you what else I'll do, too.'

He suddenly marched with purpose into the bathroom, leaving Virginia's route clear. She sped to the bed, slipped down between the sheets and huddled them round her neck. When Charlie came back he carried an aerosol tin of shaving soap.

'Guess I don't have the appropriate cream for this sort of operation, but if we need any help this might come in handy.'

He seemed to have pleased himself with his thoughtfulness. Putting the shaving soap on the bedside table, he banged his chest with his hand, making a loud clapping sound, and got into bed.

'You're a great girl, Virginia.' Virginia felt the muscles in her body tighten, and she shivered. 'Come on, now. We'll take it steady. Steady as I can.'

He turned to her with a none too steady eye, and under the sheets one of his huge, soft hands began to trace the pattern of Virginia's rib cage. He seemed to be breathing through his mouth, the breath coming in warm puffs that smelt of onion and olive and gin and whisky. In close-up his chin was pock-marked with shallow craters and there was no clear division between his eyebrows. The regularity of his features, that from a distance made him almost handsome, was lost. Virginia tried to remember the thinner, clearer version of his face in the photograph that she knew so well.

'Have you ever thought,' she asked, as his hand began to rise to her breast, 'of loving me?'

The hand stopped in mid-ascent.

'Why, now, Virginia, that's a bit early to talk about love, isn't it? We've only just met.'

'But all those years, through our letters . . . We know each other so well, don't we?' Virginia realised she sounded a little hopeless.

'Sure, through our letters we know each other probably better than a lot of people who've been married fifty years.' His voice had a terse note of agreement. There didn't seem much hope that he would expand into declarations of sudden love. And anyway, the hand was becoming impatient, pulling the sheet away from Virginia's neck. Disappointment contracted within her, increasing her tension, but she relaxed her grip of the sheet and let Charlie pull it down.

He contemplated her breasts.

'I've seen bigger,' he said at last, 'but no sweeter.'

He lowered his head very slowly towards one of them, then suddenly crashed down upon it, as if it might escape him at the last moment. The weight of his head hurt, but Virginia made no sound. She contemplated his short, bristly scalp, and remembered the carrot scalp she had been equally close to in the Welsh graveyard. If ever it was her lot to give lessons in sex education, she thought, she must remember to warn children that one of the things you could never imagine about it is the curious distastefulness of the human body in close up: the hairy dark caverns of nostrils, the ugly gash of a navel, the sticky substance of under-arm hair, the milky mess at the

73

bottom of the eyes, the three lonely hairs on a big toe, the old-knitting look of a scrotum. Close contemplation of the most perfect specimen of humanity is disillusioning. Of a lesser specimen nothing but great love or uncaring desire can protect it from being ridiculous.

Charlie was chewing her nipple. It hurt. She moved.

'That's right,' he grunted. 'Respond, honey.'

Tentatively, Virginia put a hand on his neck, which provoked nothing but a harder chew, so she slid it down his shoulder. There her fingers came upon a bristling mole: they winced away, back to the safer regions of his upper arm, and she felt guilty.

But Charlie was through with stage one. Virginia could almost see him ticking it off in his mind. He rose from her breast, contemplated her for a moment – in which she had time to take in every gaping pore of his skin, and the whole tangle of bloody veins that laced his eyeballs – then he crashed back down upon her again. This time it was to kiss her mouth. She remembered, when he smiled, she had noticed a piece of fish paté stuck between his teeth, and hated the thought of her tongue forced to be the instrument to dislodge it. Reluctantly she opened her mouth and let his tongue lash its clumsy way about. It seemed to be filling her whole head. She would suffocate, she thought, if he didn't stop soon. An ignominious way to die. She was just wondering, in a dizzy way, how her mother would explain such a death to the neighbours, when Charlie, faithful to some curious timing of his own, stopped the kissing.

He sat back on his haunches, panting. Sweat ran down the sides of his nose.

'Gee, honey,' he said, 'you're sure fiery.'

Virginia, revelling in the air that was able to swim freely through her nose again, felt that if she had been fiery then the average woman must be a nymphomaniac.

She also felt that something was strangely wrong: that it shouldn't be happening like this – she should be half drowned in an oblivion of love and desire. And here she was taking it all in quite coldly, marking up the moves with the same care she marked her pupils' homework. Perhaps, though, the ecstasy came later. At the climax, as it was called in the books she'd read.

Charlie was sitting on the edge of the bed, now, his feet on the floor. He held the tin of shaving cream in one hand and was spurting it inaccurately towards his loins. It spluttered on to his thighs and stomach. He wiped these extra bits off with one careful finger, and rubbed them into the back of his other hand. He seemed to be taking a great deal of trouble with this preparation.

'Every precaution,' he muttered, almost to himself.

He twisted his body towards her and smiled. There was considerably more hair on the left hand side of his chest than on the right. It was a darker shade of sand than on his legs, but paler than on his head. Virginia put up her hand to touch it, suddenly curious to know what it felt like.

Charlie reacted swiftly to the gesture. In one movement he got on top of her, forced her legs apart with an iron hand, and began to bluster his way into her. Immediately, it hurt. Virginia cried out.

'Stop! Please.'

'Relax, honey.'

'Please – '

'I said relax. It's going in all right.'

'It isn't. You're hurting.' Virginia could feel the shaving cream oozing down her legs and doing nothing to soothe the ripping pain within her.

'Shut up, Virginia Fly. We're doing fine.'

'Please, Charlie . . .' It came out as a whimper. A long moan followed.

'Look, who's experienced at this game? You or me? I

75

say we're doing fine. Just relax.' He spoke with the same voice as he had spoken to the untipped waiter. Then he began to gasp, and he lowered himself once more towards Virginia's mouth. Terrified that he would begin to kiss her again, she turned away her head. Too elated by now to fight, Charlie sunk his teeth into her exposed neck and scrumpled up one of her breasts in his hand as if it were tissue paper.

At this point Virginia realised there was something wrong with her. Because she knew from Caroline that it was now that you began to go wild, both of you. You lost your hold, your bearings. You soared together.

Desperately, Virginia waited for her spirit, her body, her soul, her mind to unground themselves. But here she was, watching, feeling Charlie in all his clumsy wildness, bashing away at her, groaning, covering her with his sweat and rancid breath, alone in his flight: while she remained coldly conscious of nothing but the searing pain in her vagina, the clutch of bruises in her breast, the buzz in her ears and the ache in her head. Patterns of light and shade from the satin curtains, a magnified crease in the linen of the pillowcase, Charlie's bony heel jutting out of the eiderdown – fragments of these things filled her eyes when she opened them. When she closed them she could see her virgin bedroom at home, with its dull peaceful view beyond the lattice window that no seducer had in reality stormed his way through, and she hated Charlie Oakhampton Jr. for not having managed to take her with him.

'Oh God,' she cried out loud.

'Come!' screeched Charlie, and with a final thrust and pound he gave a great shudder, and then was still. He let go of her breast, panted warm breath into her ear, and finally rolled off her. She felt his body go hot and slack against her. Her eyes were shut: he was licking saliva from his lips. Knowing she would be unseen, Virginia let her eyes trail the entire length of his body. He was quite limp now. Veiny. A streak of blood on one thigh.

'Oh boy,' he said, his eyes still shut, 'we must get some sleep. The flight's beginning to tell on me.'

He turned away from her, pulling the bedclothes over himself. Virginia was left an impossibly narrow margin of mattress. There, she would never sleep. Not that she felt one bit inclined to do so.

In a few moments Charlie began to snore, gently. Virginia slipped out of the bed without disturbing him, pulled off the eiderdown, turned off the bedside light and remembered her way through the dark to the armchair. She wrapped herself up and lay back as best she could.

She huddled there for a long time, quite awake, thinking. She realised calmly that her fantasy was over, that the bitterness of reality makes you forget that there can ever have been sweetness in anticipation. She wished Charlie had never come to England. They could have gone on writing to each other for another twelve or even twenty years, making promises to meet which never materialised, living with their imaginary pictures of each other, treating each other as a security that would never have to be put to the test of a meeting. Like that, though she wouldn't have had her bliss, he would never have faded for her: she would have loved him in a way for ever. He would have remained fair in her mind.

It was intolerably hot in the room, dry with central heating. Virginia felt that the air smelt, too, of hot salty bodies and bad breath. She went to the window but it would not open. So she went to the bathroom and decided to take a cool bath. Dirty and sore, she felt.

She could not help looking at herself in the mirror: white face, a rash like her mother's on her chest where Charlie had mauled her with his insensitive fingers, two bruises already appearing on her breast, a walnut-shaped red mark on her neck where his passionate teeth had dug into her; blood, for some reason, smeared on her stomach. What was it her mother had said? Oh yes. Quite dull girls have been known to radiate, having experienced love. Lucky, radiating, dull girls. Virginia smiled to herself.

Charlie tried to be nice in the morning, but it didn't come to him easily. He apologised for having taken up most of the bed, hoped she was all right, and went on to talk about schedules. As soon as he was out of bed he put on his blue socks and loathsome underpants, and walked about like that. Virginia was past caring.

Breakfast was brought up to the room. Charlie managed to eat the full traditional American breakfast, the sight of which nauseated Virginia, who ate nothing. She sat opposite him, in the armchair she had spent the night on, ankles primly crossed, fingering the stuff of the chair's covering. Charlie seemed not to notice her lack of spirits. He smeared a waffle with the bilious yolk of an egg, topped it with a slice of bacon and a spurt of maple syrup and ate it in his fingers like an open sandwich. Then, attempting to stop the flow of egg yolk down his chin with the back of his hand, he went to his coat – khaki-coloured, limp, at the end of his bed – and got out his wallet. He came back with it to his chair. His thumb made a yellow imprint on the mock crocodile leather. He didn't notice. Virginia watched all his movements very carefully. They meant nothing to her. His eggy chin and upstanding hair, his bandy calf and stubbly neck no longer held the power to distress her. She wondered briefly if he was about to offer her money from the fat wad of dollars he had flourished the night before.

But Charlie took from his wallet a photograph: battered, small. He handed it over to Virginia. It was in colour, taken with a Polaroid camera. A white wooden house with a green front door, and lace curtains at the windows. On the small patch of lawn in front of the house sat a fair-haired woman with a very narrow face, and two crew-cut boys, aged about five, wearing striped shorts. Virginia studied it in silence.

'Who are they?' she asked at last.

'Wife and kids.'

'Wife and kids?' Long silence.

'Yeah. Wife and kids. Back home. That's our house, see.' He leant over and tapped the house in the photograph.

Virginia felt an extraordinary sensation within her, as if her whole stomach was being squeezed. She was aware that her lips trembled across her teeth into some sort of a smile.

'You never told me,' she said.

'Yeah, well, you know. I always meant to, but I never knew how. Besides, I thought it might spoil our relationship, know what I mean?' He noticed, dimly, Virginia's dismayed face, and shrugged. 'I mean, who'd want to go on writing like that to a married man? It wouldn't be the same, somehow, would it?'

'I'd have been pleased to know,' said Virginia at last. 'I'd have been pleased for you.'

'Well, not knowing you, except like through your letters, I didn't know that, did I? There was no guarantee. So I didn't want to, like take the risk. Understand?' He looked confused himself for a moment, but brightened at the thought of a joke. 'But you know one thing, Virginia? I told Mirabelle about you, and boy was she jealous! You should have seen her.' He smiled at the memory, his voice full of self congratulation. 'Tantrums, the lot. But I wouldn't give in. "No," I said, "it's like this, Mirabelle. I been writing to Virginia Fly for seven years and I'm damned if I'm going to stop now just because we're married. She's my penfriend, and I don't want to give her up. There's nothing in it," I told her, "nothing to go off your head about. We don't have any marriage plans, Virginia and I. We're just good penfriends,"' He laughed. Virginia remained silent till the laugh petered out.

'You mean, then, that for the last five years you've been leading me to believe . . .?' Charlie was swabbing up the last of the cold egg yolk on the plate with a soggy piece of toast.

'I haven't knowingly led you to believe anything, honey, honest. I always told you the truth, just left some things out. Like when I said I kicked a ball around Saturday afternoons, I just left out that it was with Charlie junior and Denholm.'

'But you told me about *girl friends*' – Virginia emphasised the word carefully – 'girls you met in all those places you travelled to on business.'

'Sure, honey. Sure I did. That was all true. I met plenty of girls, balled a lot of them, like I said. Mirabelle and I have, like, an understanding. Now,' – he looked at her face – 'don't take on so. It's not going to make any difference to our letters, is it?'

Virginia stood up. Charlie did likewise. He put a hand on her shoulder.

'Look here, honey. I was looking forward to telling you the news. I was looking forward to seeing you, after all these years. Honest. Now I'm here, and it's great. We have a great thing going for us, believe me. I feel it all over.' He balanced on one leg, scratching the other with his foot.

'I'm afraid,' said Virginia quietly, pushing away his hand, 'I must go.'

'Where's it going to be first? The Tower?'

'No. I'm going home.'

'Now listen here, honey . . .'

'I'm sorry, Charlie. But I don't want to spoil your stay and I'd only be a gloomy companion.'

'Nonsense, Virginia Fly.' He appeared suddenly inspired. 'You're beautiful!' Virginia looked straight at him. His eyes flinched from hers.

'I'm not Charlie, and you know it. Anyhow, that's not the point. The point is, I know I'd be no good to you in the face of these – new circumstances. And anyway I have silly old-fashioned beliefs about married men . . .' She trailed off feebly.

'Very well. Any way you want it.' He stepped back. Interesting, thought Virginia, that he couldn't be bothered to make a further effort to persuade her. Had he done so, she just might have succumbed. As it was, her weekend was coming to a premature end: the time she had looked forward to for twelve years.

'Nice knowing you,' Charlie was saying, 'and don't forget, honey, you write great letters. Gee, when I get back to Mirabelle and tell her I've met you, why she'll go wild, sure as hell.' He smiled at the thought. Mirabelle's rages seemed to provoke in him some weird pleasure. 'Anyway, if you change your mind, you know where to call me. And – thanks for coming. It was a great evening, anyhow. Really great.'

'I'm sorry,' said Virginia again. 'Perhaps if I hadn't been so virginal I would have been more use to you. I wouldn't have been so – uncompromising this morning.' She managed to smile.

'There, there, now don't you worry about a thing, Virginia Fly. I'll be all right. I can look after myself, don't you worry.' He went over to the pile of travel brochures and began flipping through them. 'Dare say I'll be able to make some acquaintances somehow.'

Virginia went to the door. Charlie followed her quickly. He seemed keen for her to be gone now, so that he could get on with the business of finding someone to replace her, perhaps.

At the door, Virginia said good-bye and thank you, and she hoped he would enjoy England. They shook hands, then Charlie backed away into the room. The last Virginia ever saw of him was standing silhouetted against the net curtains, in the now familiar underpants and angora socks, pulling at the lobe of one of his long ears. Virginia reflected that the gesture conveyed a certain relief. She envied him his lack of concern, and longed for air. But her own room, four floors up, was as airless and stuffy as Charlie's had been. The bed was turned down, ready for the night before: the curtains drawn. Virginia wondered what to do. It was only half past nine. She had said she would call her mother before eleven to say if Charlie wanted to come down to lunch to-morrow. If he did, then Mrs Fly would have gone to Guildford, made the trip specially, in order to buy a superb joint. And she would make her best Yorkshire pudding, and show him the traditions of England were still worth something.

Virginia didn't ring her mother. She lay on the bed and slept immediately. She slept till three in the afternoon.

When she woke she felt hungry and cold and her head ached with a dull throb. She went downstairs looking furtively about her – she didn't want to run the risk of bumping into Charlie – and took a taxi to Waterloo Station. Charlie she thought, would be at the Tower by now, or the Zoo or the British Museum. *Dearest Mirabelle, I saw the Tower of London yesterday and two baby polar bears at the Zoo (tell that to Charlie junior and Denholm) and I met my old penfriend I told you about, Virginia Fly. Well, Mirabelle honey, you don't need to worry no more about her . . .*

At Waterloo Virginia found she had half an hour to

wait till the next train. She had £20 in her bag, saved up for the weekend. She went to the chemist and spent £5 on things she had never bought in her life before: scents, bath oils, handcreams, talcum powder, expensive soap. The thin, bulging paper bag of these things gave her a certain pleasure to hold, knowing that to-night, privately in the bathroom, she would pamper herself, soothe her body. It was a small but new kind of anticipation.

The afternoon was mild. Virginia caught the bus home from the station, enjoying her high view of the weak Surrey sun backlighting the bare trees, the muddy winter cows, the cars that crawled along the lanes at a speed which even her father would consider to be less than average.

The bus stopped at the top of Acacia Avenue. Virginia walked slowly the length of the peaceful street with its uniform houses, and respectable gardens. Through windows she saw the flicker of television sets, people crowded round the football, people who knew nothing of the experience of last night, nothing of the Piccadilly seduction of one of their quietest neighbours.

As soon as she put her key in the door, Virginia heard her mother's anxious footsteps. Mrs Fly was flushed, her eyes both worried and relieved.

'Ginny! What on earth? – I didn't know what to do about the meat. I thought you were going to ring me.'

Mr Fly appeared behind his wife.

'Are you all right, Ginny?' he asked, seeing her face.

'Yes, thank you. It's just that plans changed.'

'I said to your father: I said, "What shall I do about the meat?" Didn't I, Ted?'

'I'm sorry,' said Virginia. 'I hope you didn't buy it specially.'

'Well, I did as a matter of fact. Better be safe than sorry, I thought.'

Virginia stepped into the hall. Her parents made way for her.

'You look quite upset,' said Mrs Fly, suddenly noticing. 'Is there anything wrong? What's happened to Charlie?'

'I'm afraid,' said Virginia, 'Charlie isn't quite the man we expected. He's married.'

Mrs Fly let out a yelp of indignation. Mr Fly said 'there, there.' Then they controlled themselves and made a fuss of her. Brought her tea and chocolate cake, and turned the television on to a film she liked. Didn't ask any questions. And Virginia, exhausted, for once didn't reject the warm, dull, safe spell they wove around her. She felt in need of a welcome of any kind.

Late that night she burned the huge pile of Charlie's letters, and his photograph, in the boiler. And for several days she continued to wear a scarf, till at last Charlie's teeth marks faded from her neck, and the bruises on the rest of her body disappeared.

Chapter 5

The following Monday, Virginia asked her art class to paint a composition called 'A Bad Day.' It was keeping them even quieter than the sunsets. Louise Holcroft's head was bent low over a picture of a woman with a long sad face standing behind a blue and brown striped fence. She was scrubbing at the paper, painting the fence with great care but with a brush that was far too dry.

'More water,' said Virginia, passing on, and noticing that Louise pursed her lips. She was not a child who took kindly to advice.

Mary Edgeworth had painted a tall, ugly standard-lamp and was now at work on a pot of geraniums.

'What have they got to do with a bad day?' asked Virginia.

'They're the two things I most hate in our house,' replied Mary. 'On bad days, they show up specially.'

Virginia smiled. She liked her class. They were a good, hard-working group. Imaginative, for the most part. Curiously sensitive to her moods. She wondered what sort of a teacher she made them.

It was warm for once, in the classroom, a winter sun coming through the windows and illuminating the children's bright paintings of bad days. Virginia felt surprisingly contented. She wondered at what age you ceased to paint a bad day in bright colours. Maybe it wasn't till you were quite grown-up, or middle-aged.

She was looking forward to break with particular pleasure. In her bag were two unopened letters, and she was saving them till then. One, she knew from the hand-

writing, was from the professor. The other was the letter
she'd been waiting for, the letter she knew would come. A
rather uneven hand, vivid blue ink, postmarked Ealing
and addressed care of the television company. Someone
had seen her smile.

The bell went, shrill, echoing. The children rose immediately, at once chattering and laughing, all their concentration snapped off by the ringing peal which marked
their day, and meant now milk and buns.

'Dry your paintbrushes and put your water away, don't
forget. I want to see everything neat and tidy. Sarah,
you'll spill it if you do that. Hurry up, Lucy, can't you?
The bell's gone.'

Virginia shouted her routine admonitions. They seemed
to take an age, putting their art things away. But at last
the classroom was empty. Virginia picked up her bag and
a pile of books and walked down the clattery linoleum
corridor, which smelt of chalk and gym shoes, to the staff-
room.

This was a light, airy room overlooking a strip of well-
beaten garden, and playing-fields in the distance. The
cream walls were hung with atlases and time-tables and a
few prize poems and paintings done by former pupils. The
staff, an ill-assorted, nice crowd, stood round a trolley of
thick green cups of Nescafé, pecking at their cigarettes,
letting the smoke curl up into the air and swirl about the
beams of sunlight. When Virginia came in they turned to
her and smiled, and raised their cups, clasped in two
hands to warm their bluish fingers.

'Our celebrity! How's virgin life to-day?' Mr Bluett,
the gym and games master, poured her a cup of coffee. He
was a friendly, teasing man, pock-marked, shaggy, nearing
the age of retirement, though he didn't like to think about
that. Soon, though, the pupils would notice. Even the
simplest vault was becoming a struggle. He had always

had a certain affection for Virginia: she lent him her books of Christopher Fry and on Thursdays they had both, by mutual consent, refused the rice pudding for so many years, that at last the cook had relented and sent them up special plates of water biscuits and lumps of unfresh Cheddar. It made a bond between them.

Virginia smiled good-naturedly at Mr Bluett. Since the television programme, she had come in for a good deal of leg-pulling from the staff, and enjoyed her sudden notoriety.

'The virgin smile,' observed Miss Breedy, the maths teacher. She had made the same remark every day since the programme, and Virginia was finding it hard to respond with the same appreciation as she had done the first time. Miss Breedy was a fifty-eight-year-old virgin herself, though virgin, with its implications of fresh young things swathed in simple garments, was too light a word to apply to her. Tall and thick-limbed, moustached and frizzle-haired, she was an aggressive spinster with a surprisingly small voice. She stumped about the place singing arias from *The Magic Flute*, and in the evenings loaded herself with bags of books to be corrected in her bedsitter in Croydon. Once, guessing Miss Breedy wasn't much in demand at the weekends, Virginia had asked her home to lunch on Sunday. Miss Breedy, meticulously neat when it came to writing figures in small squares, was curiously clumsy outside the field of mathematics: she spilt her glass of sherry, her gravy, her trifle and her coffee. But she made up for it by being the first person able to make Mr Fly understand the decimal system. Virginia liked her.

But to-day she didn't want to talk to Miss Breedy, Mr Bluett or any of the others. She took her coffee to a small, low modern chair on spindly legs, in the window. Outside, everything was prematurely spring-like: a few crocuses spearing the edges of the grass, the odd snowdrop by the netball pitch. Virginia warmed her hands round her cup. When she drank she could smell the soft flowery smell of the expensive handcream she had put on them that morning. It was her new luxury and she was enjoying it. Her fingers, touching each other, felt uncommonly soft: the smell was delicious. Even Mr Fly had noticed it. He had raised his head in the air at breakfast and sniffed. What was it? Definitely not an average smell, he had said.

Virginia opened her bag and took out the professor's letter first. She slit open the envelope slowly, unfolded the single sheet of paper with care. It was only a paragraph long. Before she read it Virginia held it away from herself and contemplated the pattern the writing made. It was pleasing; the professor had fine handwriting: strong, small and neat. He managed to keep very straight lines.

My dear Miss Fly, it said, *To-night I listened to you on the television and I saw you smile. You gave a magnificent performance, considering the subject, though what on earth induced you to talk on such a thing I cannot imagine. However, I write not merely to congratulate you, but also to ask you if, before finally entering into what I believe they call an everlasting bond with your fiancé Charlie, you would spare one day out with an old friend? I have next week to go to Bolton and deliver a score, and make a lecture to some students there. Would you care to accompany me? Not a very exciting invitation, I am afraid, but whenever I have seen you off on the train, on so many evenings, I have thought to myself, one day I will accompany her on to a train. Should you accept, it would indeed be a pleasure, but of course I shall quite understand if, on Charlie's account, you dismiss the whole idea as out of hand. Yours in anticipation, Hans.*

Virginia pondered on the idea of a day trip to Bolton. She could easily get a day off school. In eight years she had only ever requested one afternoon off, for the dentist, so a second dentist appointment would cause no suspicion. But did she really want to go? She had never seen the professor, except for the one awkward lunch at home, before six in the evening. How would he appear in broad daylight? What would they talk about, in a whole day together? How many hours would it take her to tell him about Charlie, and what would she say?

Then Virginia began to imagine the pleasures of the journey: the train breakfast, a pile of unrumpled newspapers in a clean first-class carriage (the professor always disapproved of her habit of travelling second to Guildford), the fresh fields and woods streaming beyond the windows, the tall blue chimney stacks of the north: new sights and voices for a day. A little break, as her mother would say, is as good as a holiday. Virginia decided to accept.

The second letter was plump: thirteen sides of soft, cheapish paper covered with an energetic but ill-formed Biro. The writer rambled on about the excellence of Virginia's performance on television; how natural she had appeared, and yet how lonely. Virginia smiled to herself. People always connected virginity with loneliness. If you looked cheerful you were considered to be putting on a good face; look serious and at once you'd be accused of unhappiness. In fact, though much of Virginia's life had been spent alone, in every sense, she knew nothing of the sensations of lonelinesss.

The writer of the second letter ended with an invitation: *It would be so nice if we could get together. Why don't you come by Thursday week, evening, and we could go down to The George for a drink? I don't know if you care for pubs, but it's a very lively friendly place, better than my kitchen my friends say. Looking forward in anticipation to hearing from you. Yours sincerely, Rita Thompson (Mrs).*

Sudden laughter came upon Virginia. She laughed herself to scorn, out loud, sensing that behind her some of the staff shifted their positions to look at her. She could imagine their raised brows and looks of concern. Swivelling round in her chair, still laughing, she put their minds at rest.

'My first fan letter,' she explained.

Miss Breedy found herself wincing a little at the manifestations of such fame. She knotted her hands over her large bosom, privately grateful for the warmth of anonymity. Mr Bluett joined in Virginia's laughter.

'I thought you had a funny look in your eye.' He wagged his finger at Virginia, and a bell rang sharply, hurting his ears, which it never used to do.

The staff gathered up their text books and went back to their classes. Virginia was free till the 12.30 lesson. When the room was empty she got up and began collecting up the empty coffee mugs, arranging them in precise, neat lines on the trolley. Her knees felt shaky and her hands trembled slightly. Some instinct told her that Mrs Rita Thompson of Ealing would remain her only fan. There would be no more letters. For the first time for years she felt the warning signs of self-pitying tears. At once angry with herself, she hastily sat at the large round table in the middle of the room and took a pad of Basildon Bond from her bag. Above her head the last of the cigarette smoke tangled itself round the shafts of sunlight, and through the window she could see Mr Bluett, suddenly in shorts, forcing himself round the netball pitch in a measured jog.

She took up Mrs Thompson's spongy letter, re-read it, and settled down to accept its kind invitation.

Before breakfast, one morning the following week, Virginia found the professor waiting for her at the platform barrier at Euston station. He had that air about him of someone who has got up earlier than is his custom, and who has not yet fully established the kind of relationship he is going to have with the day. His tie was askew and his

grey hair in a muddle: he wore as usual his Sherlock
Holmes coat with its cloaklike shoulders, and carried a
bundle of crumpled papers under his arm.

'Ah! Miss Fly. On time as usual. Me, early as usual.
Good morning to you.'

'Good morning, Professor.'

'Please, for heaven's sake, call me Hans.'

'And me Virginia.'

Their little ritual over, they smiled uneasily at each
other. The professor took Virginia's arm and they walked
down the platform. Virginia registered the familiar bulk
of his body was comfortable. She looked forward to breakfast.

The professor had booked a table. Virginia found on her
seat a large pile of carefully folded newspapers. She took
off her coat – it was warm in the carriage – and settled
herself down happily. Hans was already disrupting the
neatness of the laid table – pushing away cutlery and
plates – to make room for his notes, which he read with
instant concentration, stopping only to cross out the
occasional word with a blunt pencil.

Virginia looked about her. She studied the hurrying
grey men on the platform, shoulders hunched, faces
serious and secretive, responsibilities packed heavily into
their fibre-glass brief-cases. She wondered whom they had
first seduced, and when, and where, and how it had been.
A tall middle-aged woman with a thin wide mouth of
scarlet, and a coat to match, came busying along with a
scattering of poodles at her high heels. She juggled their
leads with some skill, so that they didn't trip her up. She
stopped just by Virginia's window. The poodles barked
silently, and a smallish sandy man, blinking fast, caught up
the scarlet woman. They mouthed things at each other and
the man, in some agitation, dabbed at his jowls with a
string-gloved hand. The woman handed him the bunch of

leads with a flicker of a smile, and then was gone, into the train. The poodles took their chance. Instantly they zig-zagged round the man's legs, knotting him up like a may-pole. He was helpless, confused, ashamed. Just then the red woman swept down the passage between the Pullman tables, and in a careless glance noticed her man's dilemma. She stretched across Virginia's table with no apology, and opened the top window.

'Silky, Spot, Tabitha, Zeus – *Zeus*, Firle,' she shouted, 'unwind!' Poodles and man looked up at her. Poodles sheepishly unknotted themselves with some skill. 'Roger,' the woman added, '*really*. You'd better go quickly.'

She snapped shut the window. Roger, nodding, tried to wave. But as he raised the hand in which he held the leads, he succeeded in lifting three of the poodles off the ground. The woman snorted her contempt and made for an opposite table. She left behind her a sickly smell of Diorissimo which made Hans sneeze. He had not apparently otherwise noticed her scarlet shadow hanging over him.

Virginia knew how it must have been for *them*. Nineteen thirty-eight, about. Rosalind the Raver, hit of the gossip columns with her fabulous legs and cupid's bow mouth, had made her name in bright colours. Sandy, the mild gentleman with startled eyes and a willing nature, met her at the height of her successful season.

It was not long before they made the mutual discovery that each of them possessed what the other one lacked. Rosalind had life and style. Sandy had the money and the name. And somewhere or other something like love came into it.

So one night after dinner at the old Berkeley Hotel, probably, Sandy gave Rosalind a lot of champagne in his flat, where she had seriously gone to see his Matisse, and started fumbling with the fringes of her dress. Quick to take a hint, Rosalind helped him with her zip, then his flies, and they made love on the sofa. Rosalind squealed with delight, said she had never been so far before, and when could they do it again? A sudden shyness came over Sandy when it was over, and he went to the bathroom to wipe the scarlet mouths off his cheeks: but he was full of awe, too, the same feeling he had felt in chapel at school when he sang in the choir. Tears came to his eyes, and he begged Rosalind to name him any present she would like. But Rosalind was speechless, almost fainting from the exertion. He took her home in a taxi and next morning, foolish man, he sent her a poodle puppy.

Virginia smiled to herself. Poor Rosalind and Sandy now. She looked at the menu. Kippers, she thought. Kippers and *The Guardian* first, while at school they'd be singing *He who would valiant be* . . . hymn 515, Songs of Praise. She'd put it up on the board herself last night, and dusted the piano and changed the water in the glass on Miss Percival's desk, all to alleviate the guilt she felt at having told the dentist lie. The wretched Mrs Wheeler, retired, had been prevailed upon to take Class IV to-day, while Miss Fly had to go to London to have a bad time with a tooth that had been troubling her for some while. Mrs Wheeler, whose stamina was not her forte, would have to take Class IV on its monthly Nature Ramble. This was not an event Virginia ever looked forward to, what with Louise polluting the countryside with bubble-gum papers because she only liked towns, and Caroline and Lindy having competitions to see how many courting couples they could find in the scrubby Surrey hillsides. (There always were more lovers than dandelions or hips and haws, even on a Wednesday.) Mrs Wheeler wouldn't be up to it at all, Virginia knew, but she couldn't bring herself at this moment to care.

The train pulled out of the station. The rhythm of the

wheels gathered speed and she felt the warmth of sun on
her arm. She was reminded of a journey she had made
some twenty years ago, to St Ives, with her parents. They
sat opposite her, close but not touching, reading their
papers, the well-labelled suitcases and picnic basket
neatly on the rack above them. Virginia was watching the
sun spread from a narrow wedge to a great sprawling
pattern on her arm as the train drew out into the country.
Then the peace was shattered by a couple who entered
the carriage.

They were obviously just married. The girl wore a navy-
blue gaberdine suit that shone, and a pink petal hat on
top of a clump of frizzed-up hair. Paper petals stuck to her
shoulders like dandruff. Her new husband clung to her
wrist – a sweaty cheesy face with a happy nervous smile.
His other arm was dragged down by the intolerable weight
of their two suitcases, but it was no time to complain and
he kept on smiling. Mr Fly came to his rescue. He jumped
up and easily raised the suitcases on to the rack. The
bridegroom was more than grateful and Mr Fly, noticing
the young man's shaking hands, instantly set about putting him at his ease. Mr Fly's curiosity about his fellow
human beings had always, compared with the rest of his
instincts, been above average: it was no hardship to him
to ask endless questions which the newly married couple
delighted in answering. It was soon established that they
were called Sam and Adelaide Barton, and they were on
their way to St Ives for their honeymoon. This was a cue
for the Flys to remember their honeymoon, in all its dry
detail: and a cue for their bitter warning not to touch
shellfish. A bad shellfish, it seemed, had turned *their*
honeymoon (Dover in November with Mr Fly's aunt)
into a near tragedy. Though considering the failure it
must have been, they remembered it with greedy senti-
ment.

Virginia barely listened to the talk between Adelaide, Sam and her parents. She let their words fit into the pattern of the wheels until the whole thing became an agreeable pattern of sound in her head. What she remembered feeling violently, though, was envy, even hatred, for Adelaide and Sam. There they were, stupidly happy, their fingers intertwined for eight hours (they ate sardine sandwiches and bits of wedding cake with their free hands), and they had *each other* for a whole week in Cornwall, and then for the rest of their lives. Filled with childish longing for someone to love herself, she resented their happiness with her whole being. It was a tangible feeling – a dull ache from her breast bone to the pit of her stomach. To comfort herself she tried to imagine their honeymoon: at least, the sexual part of it. Caroline had recently been telling her all she knew about the weird sex life of grown-ups, so Virginia's mind was vivid with ghoulish pictures. She imagined Sam's wormish little mouth plonked on Adelaide's, and his damp fingers kneading her fleshy stomach, and his knees hacking away at her thighs to open them. She hoped it would be dreadful.

'You look melancholy, this morning, Virginia.' The professor had been looking up from his notes for some time. 'I expected you to be all sparkling. I thought engaged people sparkled.' Virginia tried a sparkling smile for him.

'I'm not engaged,' she said, in a formal voice. 'I'm nothing to do with Charlie any more, nor he with me.'

'Ah! In that case, there's no reason why you should be happy.' He summoned the waiter and ordered cornflakes and kippers for two, without asking Virginia whether that was what she wanted. Then he went on: 'From a selfish point of view, of course, that means you might be willing to come to some more concerts. I was only

95

regretting the other day that you would not be able to accompany me to Leonard Cohen at the Albert Hall in a couple of weeks time – I had great difficulty in getting the tickets. But perhaps now you will come.' He made this a statement, not a question.

'That would be nice.' Virginia bent low over her cereal to hide the blush she felt creeping over her face. Perhaps it was just the effect of having mentioned Charlie's name out loud for the first time for two weeks. 'In a few years' time,' she said, 'I shall be able to think it quite ridiculous, how it ended. For the moment, it's still rather horrible.'

'Really?' The professor didn't sound very interested.

'Piccadilly is such a dreadful place to part.' Curiously for her, she needed to tell someone just something about it. The professor's apparent lack of interest encouraged her. 'So over centrally heated, the hotel. You couldn't breathe properly.'

'If it's going to be a bad parting it might as well be in a bad place.' The professor was snarling over his filleted kipper. He would have liked to have done the filleting himself. 'My God, I remember once, I was a student in Paris at the time, this girl, Marie, how she chucked me. A great big fat blonde, she was. Huge bottom. All she really wanted out of me was a piece of music dedicated to her. She had a mortality fixation, poor bitch. Anyhow, I lusted after her, there's no doubt. One Sunday I took her down to Versailles on the train – a whole week's allowance, that, I may tell you. We walked in the gardens in the snow. Then I bought her some croissant and black cherry jam – that's how she got her bottom – and then she tells me. "Hans," she says, "this must be our last Sunday. I am off with a poet. He has written me sonnets." Silly cow. "O.K.," I said, very gruff' – he smiled at the memory of himself – ' "off you go to your poet but you must pay your own train fare back." There was a terrible confusion while she scraped about her bag looking for coins. So undignified, I thought. Then she left, waggle, waggle, munch, munch, croissant flakes falling down her breasts, and I sat there all the afternoon not really believing she'd gone. Of course, it was a blessed relief, really. But the café was so pretty, with the untrodden snow outside. That was the pity of it. She should have left me at a station or a street corner. Like that it would have been easier.'

Virginia was scarcely listening. The dull flat suburbs of Rugby were streaming across her eyes.

'I was the one who left Charlie,' she was saying, 'when I discovered he was married.'

The professor cut short any further confessions by laying a hand over one of hers.

'For God's sake, Virginia, please, spare me the details.' His eyes were ready to laugh. Virginia hesitated for a moment, suddenly saw herself as being ridiculous, and laughed at herself for a long time. The professor joined her.

They arrived at Bolton just before lunch. Virginia noticed that the woman in scarlet was met by an identical man to the man in London, except that he wore a bowler hat instead of string gloves, and led bloodhounds instead of poodles. The bloodhounds had to be restrained in their welcome. The man himself barely managed a smile. For some reason these mysterious flashes of the scarlet woman's life added to the pleasure of Virginia's day.

A student had been sent to meet the professor. He welcomed him with articulate enthusiasm, and warned him that the lecture was a sell-out. The professor expressed no surprise. He was accustomed to full halls. He puffed a bit, trying to keep up with the student. Virginia felt quite proud of him.

They went to a pub where they met a group of other

students, and an older man, German, to whom the professor delivered his score and introduced Virginia.

'Inigo Schrub, my very oldest friend, no? We were students together, for heaven's sake. Now he's risen to high ranks. Inigo is a first violin.'

Inigo laughed, his squat face reddening. He wore very round glasses. Behind them, pale magnified eyes brightened as the professor paid his compliments.

'Midland orchestra of high repute,' Hans added, and his friend's eyes dimmed right down again till they were lustreless circles of grey. But he quickly recovered himself. With an air of confused benevolence he shook Virginia's hand, bowing his head in the same manner as the professor, and thereby hiding most of his plump smile. Then he turned back to Hans and the two spoke in German. In his own language the professor spoke very fast, eloquently, Virginia felt, though she couldn't understand a word. Several times both men laughed, guttural, gruff laughs. It was the first time Virginia had ever seen the professor look as if he was thoroughly enjoying himself, and something of his enjoyment spread to her.

She studied the students round her – a long-haired, dishevelled, nice lot, in a uniform of jeans and tee-shirts and anoraks. They were kind to her, sensing her shyness; evidently impressed that she was someone in whom the professor should take an interest. They confirmed to her his popularity in the student world.

'When it's known the professor is coming,' one of them explained, 'all seats are sold out in an hour. What we have to do now is to put microphones outside the hall so that the overflow can hear.'

Virginia admitted she had never heard the professor speak.

'Then you're in for a great afternoon,' the student warned her. 'Get him on a platform and he has the entire

98

audience in his hand. And student audiences aren't that easy to please, as you must know.'

After this kind of build-up Virginia was quite prepared to be disappointed.

When drinks were over they went across to a large hall. An audience of some seven hundred was already seated, waiting. A seat had been reserved for Virginia in the front row. But she declined it and climbed alone the steps to the very back of the hall. There, she had to stand.

The stage seemed very far below. The table, the chair, the tape recorder, toy things.

Cheering started from nowhere – someone had spotted the professor in the wings. He hurried on to the stage, a tiny figure from where Virginia stood, and the cheering crescendoed. The professor seemed oblivious to the noise. His coat and notes had been abandoned, his hair flourished round his head at all angles.

Suddenly, there was silence. The professor came to the very edge of the stage. He held up his hands in a gesture of innocent surprise that he should have been asked to speak, and began.

The official title of his lecture was 'Mahler: the Man behind the Musician.' But in two hours, Virginia only remembered him mentioning Mahler twice. In fact, she realised afterwards, she would have found it impossible to summarise what he had said. She remembered the lecture only as a whole: the sweet, stuffy smell of the hall, the occasional whiff of sweat near by her; the consistent warm laughter as the professor twisted phrases into unusual structures to enlighten a commonplace observation; the extraordinary pieces of information he had acquired about the lives of various musicians – gossipy, funny, sad. When he broke off speaking to illustrate a point with a piece of music, he inevitably had trouble with the tape recorder. Each time a student had to come on and help him, and each time he waited till the student left the stage until he himself sat down, back to the audience, to listen. There was a good deal of the actor within him. Plainly he was enjoying himself, and the students loved him.

When it was over they clapped and stamped for ten minutes before leaving the hall. The professor responded with a series of understated bows. By now everyone had forgotten Virginia. Feeling uncommonly shy she made her way to the back of the stage. There she found the professor surrounded by a group of people asking questions. But he spotted her at once. Beckoned her over.

'Ah! Virginia Fly. You enjoyed it?' All eyes on Virginia. A path cleared for her to reach the professor. She felt herself blushing. Then, suddenly next to him, protected by his arm, she could smell the warmth of his body. Some flippant comment of praise was required, she felt. But she could think of none. She nodded dumbly.

'Thank God for that!' The professor laughed. 'Come. We must go for to catch our train.'

A gaggle of students went with them to the station and waved them off, urging the professor to return shortly. He made no promises, and now he was off-stage seemed no longer inspired by their enthusiasm.

'Is it always like that?' Virginia asked. They were back in the restaurant car, eating hot toasted tea cakes and drinking strong Indian tea.

'Always.' The professor had no false modesty. 'They seem to enjoy it. I can never believe they will go on wanting me back. One day I will dry up. It will all stop. I won't know how to speak to them any more.' He yawned. 'I am always tired when it's over. I can never sleep the night before – the worry of it, even after all these years. It may all appear very casual, but I have to work very hard at the preparation, you understand.'

Virginia understood. She worked hard in the preparation of classes herself. But up to now she had never been encouraged by anything like the kind of response the professor was used to receiving. In fact, for her, teaching was not a very satisfactory profession. Except in art classes she felt herself to be clumsy at communicating – The thought of classes made her wonder guiltily how the day had gone for her pupils. This morning she had felt no guilt. Strange how it came and went.

She followed the professor down the swaying corridor to the bar. Consciously, she found herself admiring his back view: the shape of his head, the cut – for all its superficial untidiness – of his grey hair, the width of his shoulders. As if aware of her thoughts he stopped, suddenly, and turned.

'One thing my wife said was that you could always judge a man by his back view.' This was the first time he had mentioned his wife to Virginia.

He continued down the corridor. Virginia had to run to catch him up. At the bar, he ordered two glasses of brandy.

'What we last drank together, if I remember?'

'I didn't know you had a wife.' Virginia was pale.

'Oh, I haven't. She's dead, for God's sake. Twenty years ago. Air crash. She and the child.' He moved his glass, which caught a reflection of the rose evening clouds, and slopped the brandy round his measure of sky. 'She was thin, like you. Quite small, too. Blonde, though. Very quiet. She would have made a good pianist one day, though she was almost too gentle. It hurt her to play *fortissimo*. I called her – the German for wood anemone.' He paused, looked directly at Virginia. 'I would have liked to have seen the child, Gretta, become a musician. She sang quite encouragingly for a child of six. She was blonde, too. The same long plait as Christabel. When they died, of course, I gave it all up too. Music, composing. There was no one else to write for. It wouldn't have been any good. Anyhow, I didn't want to, any more. But that's why I lecture, because of Christabel. She used to say to me in her music lessons – that's how we met, she was my pupil – "Oh Hans," she used to say, "you make me laugh so much I cannot play. You should make whole crowds of people laugh." As far as I could see I wasn't very amusing, but she would respond to anything I said. But I am going on to you in an indulgent fashion. Strange how people always talk in trains. You must forgive me.'

He stood up from the bar stool, formal again, his voice clipped. Again Virginia followed him down the corridor. They passed through the guard's van. Virginia touched the wire cage round the piles of mail bags. It was icy cold. She swayed a little. The light in the van was a pale greenish colour, dancing with shadows. The mail bags were piled up like rocks, stiff dull canvas stuff, horrible shapes.

Suddenly, Virginia felt short of breath. The van was airless as Charlie's room, in spite of the draughts about her legs. She cried out, clinging to the wire cage. The professor turned immediately.

'What's the matter, for God's sake?' The sight of her pale face gave him a fright. He reacted gruffly. 'Are you ill?'

'No.' Virginia tried to move but felt momentarily paralysed. The professor gave her his arm. The wheels of the train rattled a song about wives. *My wife at home my wife is dead my wife at home my wife is dead . . .*

First Charlie, now the professor. Virginia moved slowly, supported by the professor's arm. She began to cry, silently.

Back in the carriage she sniffed:

'I'm as bad as Marie, aren't I? So undignified.'

'Nonsense,' replied the professor. 'What nonsense.' He

muttered something about delayed shock, and gave her his handkerchief.

Virginia could not remember how long she cried, or what made her stop. But back at Euston she felt cheerful, if drained. The professor, who showed signs of tiredness himself, took her to Waterloo in a taxi, and then insisted on making the journey with her to Guildford. First class.

It was dark when they reached Acacia Avenue. At the porch, in the glow of the orange light, he declined to come in. Virginia was grateful. She wouldn't have wanted him to have run into her parents, then – to have been forced to answer questions about the day.

He kissed her hand and gave her one of his small, stage bows, and told her it had been a day he was unlikely to forget.

Then he stomped off down the front path, hands in the pockets of his great coat, shoulders hunched, head hung low, as if the place oppressed him.

Chapter 6

A hundred ideas had gone through Mrs Thompson's head before she eventually decided upon Ulick Brand. She had thought at first to throw a little party for Virginia Fly. But when it came down to it she realised she had neither the money, the accommodation, nor the acquaintances for the kind of party she would ideally like to give. It then occurred to her that Edgar, her brother-in-law's son, would be a suitable young man for Virginia to meet. But Edgar lived in Beaconsfield and was engrossed in his deep-litter poultry farm. He was doing very nicely at it too – he'd make a fortune, one day, Edgar. On reflection, though, he was not the most forthcoming young man Mrs Thompson had ever met, and he might think it pretty peculiar if his aunt suddenly invited him up to Ealing to meet a strange girl she'd seen on television. No, Edgar wouldn't do.

Then there was the chance she had bungled, and it still distressed her. She was at the General's flat one afternoon, typing letters to his relations in Bengal, when a young soldier came in for an interview. The General kept him waiting for half an hour while he had his afternoon doze. During that time the soldier, very handsome in his uniform, sat in Mrs Thompson's room, warming his highly polished shoes at the bar of a minuscule electric fire. Mrs Thompson abandoned her typing and decided to make friends. She chatted to him about army life, and his family, who lived at Rottingdean, and soon established he was a bachelor. She guessed his age to be about thirty. He would, Mrs Thompson quickly decided, be ideal for

Virginia. The trouble was, how to broach the subject?

She began by making him a cup of Nescafé which, she explained, was something of a risk in the General's flat because he didn't like anyone to go unauthorised into his kitchen, let alone drink from his cups. So Ronald, as the soldier was called, was obliged to feel indebted to her.

Then she plunged into the subject quite bluntly.

'If you don't mind my asking, Ronald,' she said, 'what are you doing Thursday next, evening?'

The question startled Ronald. He put the cup of illicit coffee on Mrs Thompson's desk with a bang.

'Why, I don't know. I mean . . . why?'

'Well, put it like this. I live in Ealing.' Mrs Thompson shuffled in her bag for a cigarette, and offered him one. Ronald longed to accept but thought it wiser to decline.

'Oh? I'm afraid I don't know that part of London very well.'

'It's a nice part. Trees. Coming from Rottingdean, I can guarantee you'd like Ealing.'

'I'm sure I would.' Ronald laughed nervously. Mrs Thompson fluttered her eyelashes for a moment, thoughtfully, rather than sexily, she imagined, and then gave him her most winning smile.

'I have a very special reason for asking you to Ealing next Thursday evening.' She paused while Ronald blushed. 'It would be a great personal kindness to me,' she added, 'if you would agree to come.' Appealing to him, her voice was hardly more than a whisper.

'Yes, well, thank you very much all the same, but I'm almost sure there's some military function that night. And now, if you'll excuse me, and if you'll be kind enough to excuse me to the General, I don't think I can really wait any longer. In fact, I must go.'

He hurriedly left the room without a further look at Mrs Thompson. It wasn't till the middle of that night that she woke sweating with the realisation that Ronald had got the wrong end of the stick. He must have thought she was a sex-starved old baggage, out to grasp any potential chance. She cried with shame, and cursed herself for her mismanagement.

As each new idea was reconsidered and abandoned, Mrs Thompson became more panic-stricken. The day of Virginia's visit was very near, and still she had not made any arrangements for her. In desperation she rang her friend Mrs Baxter and asked her if she could change their regular night, Tuesday, to Thursday, next week. But Mrs Baxter reacted badly to the idea. She was quite huffy. Tuesday was her day, she said, and if Mrs Thompson wanted anyone to meet her, then they'd have to be the ones to come Thursday. It wasn't up to her to change all her arrangements in order to get to Ealing on a Thursday.

In a way, Mrs Thompson was relieved. For good friend though Mrs Baxter was, she couldn't always be relied on not to speak her mind at the wrong moments. And she didn't want anyone upsetting Virginia Fly in the early stages of her strategy.

Depressed, she walked down to The George for a drink, a thing she didn't much like doing on her own. By chance, Ulick Brand, whom she'd met there several times before, was at the bar. He bought her a double gin, told her to cheer up, and they sat down at a table to talk.

Ulick Brand was a young representative of a whisky firm. He had been coming to The George quite frequently, lately, in order to persuade the landlord to display more prominently Blue Label whisky rather than that of a rival firm. The persuading meant parting with the odd fiver, but the campaign seemed to be working. Certainly a lot of Blue Label was being pushed to-night. The George would only need one more visit, then Ulick would have to concentrate his efforts on The Siren, a big pub in

Northolt, which was known not to stock a single bottle of Blue Label. This side of the business, checking on individual pubs, bored Ulick, so he fitted it in at the end of the day's work. The only thing in its favour was that at least he was able to go home feeling pleasantly drunk and uncaring.

Mrs Thompson admired him for his smart appearance – beautiful pin-striped suits and stiff collars – and exquisite manners. He appeared interested in everything she said, he bought her as many drinks as she wanted, and once he gave her a lift home in his sports car. Mrs Thompson felt quite at home with him. He reminded her of many of her clients, years ago, and she knew how to treat such gentlemen. Ulick Brand knew more about Mrs Thompson than she knew about him, it was true: with so attentive a listener it was difficult not to reminisce about all the old happy times with Bill. But Mrs Thompson managed to keep off the subject of her own life long enough to establish that Ulick lived in a freehold house in Chelsea, played squash on evenings he didn't go to pubs, and his family came from Shropshire. He never mentioned marriage, but Mrs Thompson wouldn't have been surprised if he'd once had a wife, or at least some dramatic, permanently-damaging dealings with a woman. Sometimes, he had a far-away look in his eye.

On this, her third meeting with Ulick, Mrs Thompson determined to play her cards carefully. He was her last chance. Fate had sent him to her rescue, and she could not afford to lose him.

'I have a young friend coming up to see me, Thursday,' she explained. 'Virginia Fly, she's called. Lives out near Guildford – doesn't see much of London life. I thought I'd bring her in here for a drink. I mean, it isn't like a country pub, is it?' Ulick agreed that it most certainly wasn't. 'Perhaps we'll bump into you,' Mrs Thompson went on. 'I'd like you to meet her. She's a nice girl, very quiet. Teaches.' Having come to the end of the unimportant things she knew about Virginia, she fell silent, wondering whether to disclose the most valuable bit of information. She decided to try.

'As a matter of a fact,' she went on, 'she's a very unusual girl, these days, if you know what I mean.' Ulick Brand raised his eyebrows attentively. Mrs Thompson sipped at her drink to give herself time to find the right word. 'Not – *shop soiled*. In other words' – she nodded – 'yes. At twenty-nine or thirty.'

Ulick Brand made no reply. Instead, he flipped through his engagement book. Lovely Moroccan leather, Mrs Thompson noticed. Taste.

'As a matter of a fact,' he said, so casually that Mrs Thompson couldn't make out if he'd understood her innuendo, 'I'd planned to drop in here for the last time next Thursday. I think I've got them well under control.' He smiled.

'Well! That would be nice. Something to look forward to.' In her relief, Mrs Thompson did not try to control her enthusiasm. 'I'll guarantee you'll really like Virginia – though I shouldn't raise your hopes too high, should I? But she's a really nice sort of girl.'

'I shall look forward to meeting her.' Ulick Brand had finished his whisky now and seemed in a hurry to leave. But he bought Mrs Thompson another drink to have when he had gone. She thanked him more profusely than was necessary, but the luck of it all, almost at the eleventh hour, had gone to her head.

In future meetings, Mrs Thompson decided, she would show Virginia the photograph albums, tell her about Bill, grumble a bit about Jo the lodger, have a good gossip. If she could get her up to London on a Tuesday she might even risk introducing her to Mrs Baxter. But this evening, the first evening, they would go straight to The George. She didn't want to run the risk of missing Ulick Brand, and besides, there was a good atmosphere in the saloon bar: high class, friendly. Mrs Thompson would, of course, soon put Virginia at her ease, should she turn out to be shy: but the noise, the clatter of glasses, the cosy orange lights, the shuffle of people, would all help.

Virginia arrived, in a neat grey flannel coat and woolly beret, half an hour late. In spite of her map she had got lost, and was apologetic.

'Oh, never mind, never mind,' said Mrs Thompson, who'd spent the half-hour with an anxious face behind the net curtains. 'Goodness, you're smaller than you looked on the box! I thought we'd go straight off and pep ourselves up. There's a nice place down the road.'

Slamming the front door behind her she set off fast, taking Virginia's arm across roads. It would spoil everything if they missed Ulick Brand.

But he was standing in his usual place at the corner of the bar. Mrs Thompson gave a convincing little start, clapping her hand over her mouth.

'Oh, my! There's a friend already. What a coincidence.' She introduced Virginia to Ulick, who immediately bought them drinks, and they sat down at a table.

Mrs Thompson saw to it that there should be no moments of awkwardness, or silence. She chatted on, barely pausing to drink, about the old people's panto-mime and Mrs Baxter's mother who was to be put into a lunatic asylum next week. Virginia watched her atten-tively – the tired, lined eyes, bright with make-up, darting about the place, the dry hair tortured into waves, the brooch of imitation emeralds on her lapel. She wondered why Mrs Thompson had written to her: what she wanted from her, and whether this would be their first or their last meeting. She had a headache and felt tired. The man with the black moustache had been disturbing her sleep again, and she'd been writing end of term reports till late at night. She wondered when and how the evening would end.

Ulick appeared to be listening to Mrs Thompson with great attention. Occasionally he glanced at Virginia, noticing her pale face and the shadows, same grey as her coat, under her eyes. Not his type. He was attracted to large, healthy women with shining hair and big teeth, and large bra-less breasts and bright clothes. This girl, Virginia, looked as if she'd been born in the wrong century, a sort of sub Jane Eyre. And yet there was something faintly arresting about her stillness, her melancholy.

With every drink Mrs Thompson became more adventurous in her reminiscenses. The chatter that began as a way to ease an unconventional meeting became, on her part, an indulgence in nostalgia. She made Ulick and Virginia smile.

'Ah! In the old days – I was a slim young thing then – I drank nothing like this. Tea was my time. The Ritz – I will always remember tea at the Ritz. You, of course, Ulick, will be well acquainted with the Ritz.' Ulick raised his eyebrows. Mrs Thompson didn't wait for any affirmation of this comment, but went on: 'I will always remember, one summer's day, tea at the Ritz with Freddie Colhoun – there, now I've let the cat out of the bag, haven't I?' She giggled. 'We sat under a palm tree and drank china tea with lemon, and Freddie had an ebony cane that he scratched his chin with. A nervous habit, I suppose. He said I had stars in my eyes, and yet he wouldn't take me to his flat. He was a one, Freddie. Very cautious. I often tried to persuade him to be a bit more daring. "Come on Freddie," I used to say. "Snap out of it. Let's go somewhere, one of the smart clubs, and

dance and sing and show people we're happy." But he
never took to the suggestion. He liked to come and visit
me at my flat, best – I had a lovely place in the West End
– and bring me little surprises. A bottle of perfume or a
jar of Russian caviar, very generous. But then of course
he was stinking rich. You could tell just by his cuff links.'

She paused, glancing at Ulick's wrists. A flicker of gold
reassured her.

'As a matter of a fact, that tea at the Ritz was the last
time I ever saw Freddie. He didn't seem to enjoy the
afternoon as much as I did. I was laughing, and chucking
him under the chin, flirting a bit, you know, trying to
bring him out of himself, and he kept looking at the
waiters. In the end he said they were all looking at me.
He was that sensitive! Silly old fool. He just crawled back
into his shell like a silly old crab, and sent me roses next
day saying he was off abroad. I read somewhere he died
in a car crash, it must have been just after the last war.
They said he was the owner of a big racing stable. He
never told me that, but men never guess what you
might be interested in, do they?'

At nine o'clock Virginia began to agitate about her
train home. Any flicker of anticipation she had had about
the evening had been dulled. Ulick Brand epitomised the
kind of man with whom she had nothing in common and
Mrs Thompson, for all her kindness, was tiring. You
needed to be in the right mood for her.

Ulick Brand, who scarcely covered his eagerness to
make his departure, too, offered Virginia a lift to the
station. She accepted. On the way they dropped Mrs
Thompson home. For her part, she was happy. What with
the gin, and the prospect of her plans materialising so
soon in a way which even she had hardly dared hope for,
she did nothing to contain her squeaks and giggles of joy
as they let her out at the door.

'Take her straight to the station, Ulick, and no misbehaving!' She wagged a warning finger. Virginia
blushed.

Ulick had no intention of misbehaving with Virginia
Fly, but he was hungry. He was faced with three alterna-
tives: two deep frozen rissoles in his fridge, dinner alone
in the local bistro, and he was very tired of their stroganoff,
or dinner with Virginia, should she accept. He glanced at
her. She was pulling on black wool gloves with fleecy
cuffs.

'How would you like some Chinese food before going
home?' he asked.

Virginia, in a driftwood mood, happy to be moved
along by anyone else's whim, said yes she would like
some Chinese food. With no further conversation they
drove to a restaurant in Knightsbridge, all tiled floors and
low lights hanging over the tables. The place seemed to
be full of people dressed in magnificent flowing clothes
from Afghanistan, embroidered shirts and flaming
velvet jeans; their hair tricked into corkscrew curls, their
feet booted or bare. Several of them nodded at Ulick as
he led Virginia to their table. As soon as they sat down
she pulled off her gloves and coat. Beneath it she wore an
embroidered blouse her mother had bought at Zurich
Airport – at least, among all the colours of the other
diners, it made her feel less conspicuous than her dull
grey coat.

Ulick stretched an arm over the table and pinched her
cheek.

'You're the palest girl I ever saw. Quite bloodless. Are
you always like that?' She noticed, when he smiled, he
had nice, even teeth, very white, and the lines by his
mouth crinkled in a way that was rather endearing. Perhaps he wasn't so bad after all, though if there was one

thing that made Virginia uneasy it was to ask her a direct question about herself.

The usual childish flush crept up her face. Still unable to control it, she knew the only way to minimise its effect was to smile. The result pleased Ulick.

'That's better. Now your face is working. You look like a proper person who's been out in winds and sun, not like something just out of the deep freeze.'

Virginia laughed. She was suddenly hungry. Ulick ordered for her – little shrivelled up things she'd never seen or heard of before that looked lost on the huge white plates. To hide their nakedness, she covered some of them with clumps of fried seaweed, then gave herself all the pleasure of tearing the clumps apart to re-find the bean-shoots and shrimps that she had just hidden. Ulick watched her carefully, amused. He refrained from asking her if she was well acquainted with Chinese food.

Instead, he talked about Mrs Thompson, and after two glasses of sharp, icy white wine, Virginia told him how their meeting came about. Ulick managed to conceal any amazement he may have felt. Instead, he kept on the subject of Mrs Thompson.

'She must be a lonely old cow to do such a thing.'

'She was being kind. Perhaps she thought she could help me.'

'What sort of help does she think you need?'

'I don't know. Perhaps she just couldn't resist thrusting upon me some of the help she felt like giving. You know what they are, those people who need to give help. They fling it about regardless.' A little uncertainly she recalled something she had been reading. 'You know what Proust said? He said that we pack the physical outline of the creature we see with all the ideas we have already formed about him, and in the complete picture of him which we compose in our minds these ideas have principal place. So if Mrs Thompson, seeing me on television, gets it into her head that I need help, and that very idea does something to benefit her, then nothing in the world is going to change her mind.'

She spoke shyly, uncertain whether or not she should have mentioned Proust. Ulick did not give the appearance of being a literary creature: he might think she was trying to score over him.

Instead, quizzically, he pushed back his chair and looked at Virginia with something that could have developed into interest, had he allowed himself to continue the thought.

'I haven't read Proust, as a matter of a fact. Dickens was my only "heavy." I only have time for Chandler, and not much even for him, these days.' He spoke with the superiority of those whose lack of time makes the people who find the time to appreciate any form of art sound guilty. Virginia was snubbed. She blushed again, unable to hide from the gaze which Ulick continued to inflict upon her. He lit a cigarette, very fast – he seemed to do everything, but speak, very fast – and stuck it in an amber holder. Then, to ease her, he smiled.

'Don't say, Virginia, you're searching for an identity? God, that's so tiring. I know so many girls who do. They look quite exhausted.'

'Who said anything about identity?' Virginia heard herself sounding quite snappy.

'Nobody. I was just wondering to myself why you looked so tired.'

'I'm not tired. You mustn't concern yourself so.'

'Oh, I have very little concern, not enough concern. That's one of my weaknesses.' He blew a cloud of smoke above his head, in such a way that as it began to disintegrate it moved away from Virginia. 'Mrs Thompson told me you come from Surrey.'

'That's right.'

'I could almost have guessed.'

'Is that meant to be insulting?'

'Not exactly. It's just that there's something about Surrey girls. I went out with one, once, years ago. She lived on the outskirts of Guildford. She was exquisitely preserved. For twenty-three years no one had managed to undo the knot in her Hermes' scarf. Of course, now, she's been divorced twice and is on heroin, poor thing.'

Virginia straightened her back, supported her chin on clenched hands, and looked very serious.

'Well, I know a girl from near Guildford who was a virgin till she was thirty-one, and then was raped by an American penfriend in Piccadilly Circus.'

'Really?' said Ulick disbelieving. 'It just shows you what a disadvantage you are up against. How careful you must be.' He looked at his watch. 'And talking about being careful, you've missed the last train.'

She had. It was well past midnight. But Ulick was the one who appeared, contrary to what he had recently said, most concerned.

'Hadn't you better ring your parents?'

'Oh, them.' Virginia's head was a globe of moving liquid. She summoned up two words she had never used in her life before. '*Stuff them*. They must learn that I'm grown-up, now.'

Ulick smiled, perhaps appreciating what the observation must have cost Virginia.

'Well,' he said, 'there's a spare room in my house. You're welcome to use it.'

Virginia began to search her seat for her gloves.

'Thank you,' she said, trying to divide the words. 'That's-really-very-kind-of-you.'

Ulick's house was one in a terrace of tall, narrow façades

of elegant proportions. In the minuscule courtyard that
protected it from being jammed against the pavement
grew an old wisteria tree, its geriatric branches, jewelled
pathetically with fresh leaves, climbing round the two
windows on the ground floor. The tree, Virginia felt sure,
identified Ulick's house as being quite the most expensive
in the terrace.

Ulick turned the lights on in the hall. It was a tall,
narrow area, dense with thick carpets and silky walls. A
pile of unopened letters and newspapers lay on a polished
table. There was a smell of air that had been dried out by
central heating, of air that had no chance to be re-
invigorated by the flashes of wind or sun that came
through the briefly opened front door.

Ulick flicked through the letters.

'Nothing that can't wait. Let's have just one drink
before bed.'

He bounded up the narrow stairs. Virginia, following
him, felt each stair to be extraordinarily squashy, padded
with its thick pile carpet, beneath her feet. A curious
sensation she had never felt before. At home the stairs
were hard things, their bones merely covered, not dis-
guised, by thin haircord.

The drawing-room, like the hall, was a narrow dark
place, swags of grey silk curtains at each end, mahogany
bookshelves reaching to the ceiling, lights so subdued that
you had to search for their source. Ulick was at a plate-
glass table pouring drinks: someone had put ice in the
silver bowl. Virginia stood some yards from him, ankle
bones touching, both hands on her bag, hoping that he
would not make the whisky too strong.

'This is awfully grand, for a bachelor,' she said.

'It is, for a bachelor.' Ulick turned to her, holding out a
glass that was so thick and nubbled with intricate designs

that it scraped her hand. 'For God's sake, take that dreadful coat off. It reminds me of my spinster aunt.'

He said it nicely, but in her confusion Virginia had to return the glass to him before she could take off the coat. At last, feeling naked in her Zurich blouse, she stood apart from him again, the fierce glass cradled in both her hands, wondering what to do. In spite of the central heating, she shivered.

'Tell you what, I'll play you a tune.'

Ulick went to the shining grand piano, sat on the velvet stool, and ran his hand along the keyboard, looking for dust. Virginia moved to the fireplace. Its marble was scooped into designs as complex as those on the glass: she ran a finger along the stamens of a cold lily, and shivered again.

Ulick was fiddling among the notes.

'I used to play for hours every day. Hardly any time now.' Again, he made his busy life sound like something he was proud of rather than something he regretted. 'Anyway, I like playing to people. I'm an awful show-off.' He swung choppily into some tunes of the Twenties, humming just off key, occasionally substituting the hum for a few remembered words.

Virginia, at the fireplace, took a drink, put down her glass, and began to swing one leg, from the hip, in time to the music. Ulick watched her.

'You've got nice legs,' he said. 'And you look as if you once practised at a bar.'

'I did. I wanted to be a ballet dancer, once, after seeing *The Red Shoes*, years ago. I took lessons. In Guildford, of course.' Her grey flannel skirt, in spite of its inverted pleat, constricted her movements. She hitched it up over her knees. 'In my mother's eyes, I was second to Fonteyn after three lessons. But a year later they told me I'd never make it. I was too stiff. "You mustn't *strap-hang* on to the music," my teacher said. "You must *flow* with it." I realised I'd never learn to flow, so I gave up.'

Ulick continued playing, watching Virginia's thin calf and thigh in its stringy tights swing like a metronome in time with his honky-tonk music.

'What did you want to be then?'

'A tap dancer, next, after I saw an old Fred Astaire film.'

Ulick changed key into 'I've Got You On My Mind' and Virginia shuffled a little on the marble hearthplace, her heels making hardly audible clicks. Then she spun out from her stage, arms out, moth-like, and twirled to the piano. There, panting a little, she folded her arms on its top.

'Oh, I can be quite gay, sometimes,' she said. 'Isn't it ridiculous, two drinks or more – well, more than two *mixed* drinks, and I want to dance. I think I must be thoroughly drunk.'

'I like you drunk, then,' said Ulick.

'And when I'm even a little drunk,' Virginia went on, 'which isn't very often, honestly, then I feel more than ever my sense of the chameleon. I feel that wherever I am, whoever I'm with, I become a part of, totally. It's an effort, at those times, to believe that really I'm Virginia Fly, from Acacia Avenue, Surrey: mediocre school teacher, loyal daughter, monotonous life and so on. I am a part of the present.' She paused, thinking. 'So at the moment, it's impossible to believe that this room isn't familiar, that I haven't lived here for years, not *with* you, but *as* you . . .' Ulick had stopped playing and was listening. 'I mean, just from showing me a few of your – things, and talking to me for a while, I can imagine so exactly your life that momentarily it seems as if it's my own.'

'A very old form of escape,' said Ulick, 'you'll grow out of it.' He touched her cheek, more kindly than in the restaurant. 'At least, you've got some colour in them now. All that dancing.' He stood up and banged down the piano lid. 'Bed,' he said.

Virginia followed him upstairs, where the carpets were just as thick as downstairs. He led her to a small box of a room whose walls and ceiling were covered with dark brown felt. One wall appeared to be entirely cupboards: the felt was nailed to their seams with hundreds of small brass knobs. The curtains and carpets were burnt orange, the cover of the bed tailored tweed. It all smelt expensive.

'My dressing-room,' explained Ulick. 'I hope you'll be all right. Bathroom's first on the left.' He rubbed the top of her head. 'I'll be gone long before you wake up in the morning, so help yourself to breakfast.'

'Thank you,' said Virginia, 'but I won't bother. And thank you for dinner, too.'

Ulick stood at the door, a yard away from her. She felt cold again.

'There are Disprin, should you want them in the morning, in the bathroom cupboard.' He smiled. 'And thank you for dancing for me.' He shut the brown felt door.

Alone in the room, Virginia looked for signs of Ulick. But for one ebony-backed hairbrush, there were none. She pulled back the bedcover. Orange sheets matched the curtains: shiny, cold. Initials on the pillow cases. She undressed. Then, naked, enjoying the feel of the soft carpets on her bare feet, she crept over to the cupboards and opened one of the doors. A light snapped on as she opened the door, illuminating a crowded rail of suits: dark, light, tweed, velvet – seventeen. She counted them. In another cupboard were shelves of silk shirts, pale sugared-almond colours at one side, shirts of a more flamboyant nature on the other. Also, seventy-one beautiful ties and eleven pairs of supple leather shoes.

All the cupboard doors open at once now, Virginia sat

on the bed and stared at the collection before her. She sighed. In her father's cupboard there were the three suits she knew well: his summer best, his winter best, and his everyday grey. Four or five ties, three pairs of shoes. Here, it was like a shop.

'Like a bloody shop,' she said out loud. She slammed shut the doors but they made no noise. Then got into bed. But she was wide awake. On the bedside table were three books: *The Concise British Flora in Colour*, *The Millionaire Mentality* and something by Chandler. She settled for the flowers.

A few moments later she thought she heard Ulick shutting a door along the passage. Her heart quickened; her feet, suddenly very hot, scrambled about to find a new area of cool sheet. She watched the brass handle on her own door, waiting for it to turn, but it didn't move. Without bothering to get out of bed, as was her normal custom at home, she muttered a variation on her usual prayer: *Please God, I would like him to come back, and be gentle with me. Please God: after all, he liked my legs . . .*

But he didn't come, and Virginia grew tired of waiting. She resigned herself to the study of British flora for most of the night.

The next morning, in Ulick's small, dazzling kitchen, Virginia found a note saying he hoped she'd had a good night and would make herself a decent breakfast. He added that he would like her to leave her telephone number, and here was a pound for a taxi to the station. It was his fault she had missed the train.

The sun in the kitchen hurt Virginia's eyes, and her head throbbed. In spite of her last night's statement about not bothering with breakfast, she boiled the one cold white egg she found in the enormous, almost empty fridge, and made herself some black instant coffee. The kitchen, she saw through flickering eyes, was as impersonal as the other rooms she had seen: no apron on the nail, cookery books, old shopping lists or grocery bills. It was as if someone had come into the house and swept away every trace of anything that might give a clue to the owner's character. Or perhaps Ulick had simply called in a decorator and given him *carte blanche*, but the decorator hadn't felt it was part of his job to supply the paraphernalia of his clients. Virginia wondered about Ulick. Unlike last night, when she remembered so well the sensation of being him, of knowing what it was like to live in this house, she now felt both he and it were all strange to her. She was curious about them, but she wanted to go.

When she had finished the tasteless egg, she wrote *thank you* on the Formica table with her eyebrow pencil, and left the money by the words. She put on her gloves, and shut the thick front door behind her. In the bright sunlight the wisteria tree now looked even more expensive than it had done at midnight. Something about it made Virginia change her mind, and abandon the idea of the taxi she had intended to take. And so, shocked at first by the hardness of the pavements, after the luxury of Ulick's carpets, she began the long walk to Waterloo Station.

Chapter 7

Virginia Fly did not share the same enthusiasm as her
pupils for the holidays. To her, they were a tedious break.
Term-time was hard, monotonous work, but at least it
protected her from her mother's day-long observations.
And this holidays, what with the break-up with Charlie,
Virginia's new friend Mrs Thompson, and the mysterious
night Virginia had spent in London, Mrs Fly had much
to muse upon out loud.

It was Virginia's custom to set her pupils A Holiday
Task, and in the same way she solemnly set herself A
Holiday Pleasure. This holidays the pleasure was to be
Middlemarch and Van Gogh's letters. The books gave her
some measure of escape, but not much. Almost as soon as
she had settled down to read in her room after breakfast,
her mother would call up to her:

'Coffee, Ginny?'

'No thank you.'

'Everything all right?'

'Yes thank you.'

'Fancy cottage pie for lunch?'

'Lovely.'

'I can't hear.'

Virginia would put down her book and go to the top
of the stairs.

'I said lovely.'

'I'm just off to the shops, then. Anything you want?'

'No thank you.'

'Take care.'

But even Mrs Fly's shopping meant not more than half an hour's peace. She preferred to go to the shop at the end of the road three times a day to get a few things every time rather than make one major expedition. Both her husband and daughter had pointed out to her that this was an uneconomic way of reserving her energies, but it was, she said, her way of doing things. She had always shopped like that, nothing would change her now, and anyhow she liked the little walks.

So when, unbearably soon, the small, sharp efficient pecking noises that Mrs Fly made in the kitchen started up again, Virginia slammed shut her book and decided to go for a walk. To relieve her mother of any anxiety she would have been bound to have felt had she found her daughter's bedroom empty, Virginia made an effort to go through the kitchen.

'I'm going for a short walk before lunch.'

Mrs Fly was releasing her meagre purchases from their string bag; half a pound of mince, a pound of potatoes, a tin of apricots.

'Well, I've bought mince, potatoes, and apricots for a nice flan. That should see us through till this evening. Take care you don't catch cold, now. There's quite a nip in the wind.'

Virginia walked through the garden to the field. The pale April sun was quite warm and the breeze, far from being malicious, was barely strong enough to bow the few anaemic daffodils that had survived Mr Fly's ruthless methods of gardening.

She took her usual walk: up the beaten path over the mild hillock, which she half despised because of the tameness of its form, and into the spinney. Everywhere the bracken was beginning to uncurl its small fists of bright green; the litter of last summer had rotted with the autumn leaves and there was a stirring of birds in all the branches. Virginia had taken the same walk hundreds of times, in all seasons, and yet still found herself almost as surprised and delighted by the changes as she had been as a child.

A huge oak tree at the highest point of the spinney marked the end of this routine walk. Years ago, its branches had been her secret retreat. She had spent many an afternoon with a book high up in a rustling green world that no one could find, content just to look at the changing patterns of sun on the leaves. Nowadays the lower half of the tree, at any rate, was no longer undiscovered. The Council had put up a sign on a nearby main road urging motorists to the 'picnic area' at its feet, and as further encouragement they had provided a wooden bench and table, and a litter bin. But for the moment the area was deserted, the litter bin empty. She went over to the trunk of the tree, put her hand on a space of uninitialled bark, and looked up at the huge tower of branches, hazy with new leaves.

'Virginia Fly,' she said out loud, 'what is going to happen to you?'

For as long as she could remember, Virginia had, on occasions, asked herself questions out loud. They were always questions she was unable to answer, and it never occurred to her to try to answer them. To ask was consolation in itself. Feeling quite cheered, and a little ridiculous – as she always did, having asked herself such a question – she left the picnic area and thought of Ulick Brand's wisteria tree.

The return walk was not half such a pleasure. For as soon as she was out of the spinney and descending the dip – you couldn't call it a valley – there was the view of the back of Acacia Avenue's ugly houses, fluttering their little strips of garden behind them, nestling up to their gloomy bushes of laurel and rhododendron. Going for the walk you could almost imagine you were in the country. Returning, the illusion was impossible.

Every day of the holidays Virginia dreaded lunch alone with Mrs Fly. The meal left her vulnerable to all her mother's wildest suspicions, suppositions and speculations. To-day, Ulick Brand was on her mind.

'What did you say was the name of the Chinaman you went out with a couple of weeks ago?' She helped Virgina to the crustiest part of the potato to soften the inquiry.

'I didn't say he was Chinese. I said we went to a Chinese restaurant.'

'Well, not that I'd mind of course. You know me, broad-minded to a fault – as long as you don't bring home a Chinaman as a husband.'

'I don't know any Chinamen, so that's not likely.'

'And anyhow, I've never been able to see the attraction of all that chop-suey food, myself.'

Irritated by her mother's stubborn train of thought, Virginia broke the ensuing silence.

'I said the man I had dinner with that night was a friend of Mrs Thompson.'

'Oh, blow me! So you did. What a memory. I get so muddled with all your friends.' She dug at the corner of her mouth with a tiny corner of her napkin, wiping away flecks of mince meat which had gathered there. The refinement of the familiar gesture drove Virginia to such fury that over the years she had trained herself to look away as soon as her mother picked up her napkin from her lap. 'Talking of Mrs Thompson,' Mrs Fly went on, then paused. She picked up her glass of water and took a sip so small that, poured out, it wouldn't have filled half a thimble. To add weight to the importance of her news Mrs Fly continued her silence for some moments.

'Talking of Mrs Thompson,' she said again, at last, 'she

rang up this morning. You were on your walk.' She waited for some reaction from Virginia, but it didn't come.

'She asked how you were, of course, and wondered if you would be up in London again soon. She wanted you to go round for a meal. We had quite a little chat.' She paused. Virginia took a long time to lever an apricot out of its custardy bed.

'Oh? I'll ring her back this evening.'

'No need,' said Mrs Fly. 'She's coming down here Sunday for the day. I asked her. I mean, I thought you'd be pleased, and your father and I would like to meet her. We like to meet your friends.'

Virginia said nothing, but looked straight at her mother. This time there was custard in the corners of her mouth.

'I wish you wouldn't make arrangements with my friends,' she said, finally.

'But I thought you'd be so pleased. I was only doing what I thought best – '

'Quite. You always do what you think best.'

'I shall enjoy meeting Mrs Thompson. There must be something very good-hearted about a person who writes to someone they've seen on television and asks them out.'

'You may not like her. She's not exactly your kind of friend.'

'What do you mean by that?'

'Her appearance is a bit flamboyant for you. And she talks a lot.'

'Just because I'm not an extrovert dresser myself, that doesn't mean to say I don't admire it in other people.' Mrs Fly searched out the two remaining clean corners of her napkin to deal with the custard. 'Well, we shall see.'

Far from being daunted by Virginia's warnings, Mrs Fly was more determined than ever to like her daughter's friend. Prejudice set in. By Saturday it would have congealed to the point that, whatever kind of character Mrs Thompson turned out to be, she could be assured of a great welcome from Mrs Fly.

Most of the week Mrs Thompson spent in a dither of happy anticipation. She rang her friend Mrs Baxter almost hourly to discuss finer points of the outing, and on Tuesday night, their regular night together, could talk of nothing else. Mrs Baxter, for her part, was unusually tolerant. She was jealous of Mrs Thompson's coloured wine glasses, old ermine cloak and signed book of war memoirs by her employer the General. But she was not jealous of a day in Surrey: it was something she'd go out of her way to avoid. Anything beyond Barnes was a wilderness to her: she couldn't be sure unless she had a solid pavement under her feet. However, if the idea of a day with the Flys, whoever they may be, gave Mrs Thompson any pleasure – and indeed she did seem to be unusually flushed with excitement – then she Mrs Baxter wasn't one to damp her spirits. Besides, it made a nice change of conversation.

By instinct Mrs Thompson was no more a country lover than Mrs Baxter. She had little experience of the country: the odd roadside picnic with Bill on Bank Holidays, a couple of weekends with a farmer uncle in Worcestershire, a terrible tour of the Lake District with her elderly mother – none of these occasions she remembered with pleasure. Her present worry, faced with a rural day, was what to wear. Her wardrobe didn't include any tweeds or brogues which, she felt, would have been appropriate. And Mrs Baxter was hardly a constructive help.

'You don't want to stand out too much against all those greens,' she advised. Surrey was a jungle in her mind. 'And you don't want to wear a feathered hat. It frightens the birds.'

'How about my rust jersey?' Mrs Thompson held a dying dress against herself, posing in front of her long mirror. 'I could dress it up with my coral spray.'

'You don't want to dress it up with anything, dear,' said Mrs Baxter. 'They dress down in the country, not up, I'm telling you.'

'You're quite right,' said Mrs Thompson. This was a big concession on her part. The zest in her relationship with Mrs Baxter was always to ask advice, but never to accept it. 'You're quite right. I'll dispense with jewellery for the day.' Mrs Baxter was made almost speechless by the rare event of her friend agreeing with her. Her voice went quite weak:

'Well, you *are* right, dear. Like I said, it wouldn't do anything for you, jewellery wouldn't, in the country.'

It was one of the best evenings they had ever spent together.

Later, Mrs Thompson hung the rust jersey outside her cupboard, ironed it several times, polished her brown shoes, renewed the solid powder in her compact, set her hair and didn't complain when Jo the lodger turned up his hi-fi too loudly. She wouldn't admit it, even to Mrs Baxter, but for some reason she felt excited as a child.

Sunday morning Ted Fly finally broke to his wife something he had been feeling all week: that to-day was a good day to go down to a place he knew in Hastings to look for a second-hand mowing-machine. Mrs Fly was incensed.

'But *Mrs Thompson*'s coming.'

'I know.'

'To-day of all days to choose to see a mower. She's coming down from *London*, you know.'

'I'll fetch her at the station. Just go off for a bit once she's settled.'

'Haven't we been talking about her coming all week?'

'You have.'

'Well, then. Really. What will she think?'

'She'll think I've got to go and see a mower.' Mrs Fly sniffed. Some instinct told her husband not to weaken. 'There's a lovely machine going there for £10. It would be silly to miss it . . .' He wouldn't give in, but his wife's face troubled him, all the same. 'I'll be back in time to take her back to the station, don't worry.'

'I should think so too.' Mrs Fly slammed her knitting down on to her wide-slung knees. She found it difficult to lose battles graciously. But once Ted had become obstinate about something she knew there was nothing further she could do to make him change his mind. Well, more fool him, if he wanted to miss such a pleasant day.

As soon as she had got into his car, Mr Fly put his case to Mrs Thompson. He made it abundantly clear to her that, sad though it was, his journey to Hastings was imperative. The price of gardening equipment was going up all the time, and he'd be an idiot to miss such a snip, wouldn't he? Mrs Thompson agreed he would. He was so charming, so concerned, Virginia's father – probably the one from whom she'd inherited her nice quiet ways. Not for one moment would it have occurred to Mrs Thompson that her host's urgent journey might have any suspect motives. He seemed the perfect gentleman.

In fact, by going away for the best part of the day, Mr Fly was only trying to make things easier for everyone. He had learnt from experience that, when his wife had a friend in for the day, his own day became a thing not to be considered. His presence seemed to annoy. His views, if asked for, were automatically contradicted. Even his offers of help – washing up, making tea, anything – were spurned. As soon as the friend left, of course, things returned to normal. Mrs Fly nagged and soliloquised, but was warm again. It never occurred to her that she had been in any way different while she entertained. Generous in his solutions, Mr Fly put down her strange behaviour to nerves. She didn't know what she was doing. Still, it was confusing and, in the old days, hurting. So he had found the answer: make an infallible excuse to go out, and stick to it. In fact, as far as he could judge on the journey from the station, Mrs Thompson was a nice woman. Understanding. Must have been rather good-looking, once, too. For a moment he felt regretful about having been so insistent about the mowing-machine. But as soon as his wife met Mrs Thompson and guided her, touching her arm, into the sitting-room, that moment passed. No one said good-bye to him. He hurried away.

Mrs Fly had planned everything with customary precision. Presuming that the train wouldn't be late, and guessing that her husband's speed back from the station would be average, she managed to have the coffee percolator boiling just as the car drew up at the gate. She sped with her beautifully laid tray (frilly napkins, Dresden china, iced shortbread biscuits, little forks just in case – a credit to any butler) to the sitting-room, then arrived calmly at the front door just as Mrs Thompson came through the gate.

Although she knew that her guest lived in Ealing, Mrs Fly had convictions, based on no factual evidence, that Mrs Thompson was born, bred and used to a better part of London. Somewhere near Belgrave Square or Buckingham Palace, she imagined. Of course, a lot of people were moving out of the centre nowadays: it was understandable. And Mrs Thompson, being a widow, was probably not as well off as she had once been. Still, wherever she lived now, Mrs Thompson – you could tell just from the way she walked up the path – was a woman of *breeding*. Mrs Fly pursed her lips ready to break into a smile of welcome. She would see to it that Mrs Thompson felt at home.

Mrs Thompson, for her part, was finding pleasure in every moment. Both Mr and Mrs Fly, and their house, exceeded her expectations. Everything was warm and neat. The atmosphere filled her with well-being. What's more, the choice of the rust dress had been right: Mrs Fly herself was also in a jersey dress, olive green, with a small opal brooch at the neck. This caused Mrs Thompson's only regret: she shouldn't have listened to Mrs Baxter about the coral spray. She should have worn it. But still. It was a small thing.

The two women sat side by side on the tweed-covered sofa, the sun shone on the Dresden and there was a strong smell of carnation scent that came from Mrs Thompson. Virginia, opposite them in an arm chair, could not help smiling at the contrast they made. If she half shut her eyes their heads were two strange balloons hanging from the ceiling – one, with a blurred, indistinguished sort of face, powdery round the mouth, brown hair rolled up at the ends like a document. The other, a bright, clinical face, hardened rather than softened by its careful make-up, downward lines round the mouth, a yellow puff of fibre-glass hair, a crumpled neck. The heads bobbed about smiling at each other: Mrs Fly's smile was of melon pink gums frilled with pearly false teeth. Mrs Thompson's was more rugged. Her plum lipstick made her own teeth seem less ochre than they really were, and when she laughed a flash of gold fillings and bridges revealed the precarious state into which they had fallen.

'Isn't this funny, how it all came about?' she was saying. 'You never know, do you?'

'You never know,' agreed Mrs Fly.

'And what's become of – I've been dying to ask – what's become of Virginia and Ulick?' Mrs Thompson addressed the question to Mrs Fly, not looking at Virginia.

'Ulick? Ah yes. The Mr Brand. I get so muddled with her friends, don't I Ginny? What's become of Ulick? – They went to a Chinese restaurant, you know. Ginny *chose* it, she said. I don't know how anybody finds those little helpings satisfying.'

'Nor me,' said Mrs Thompson. She turned to Virginia. 'Come along, Ginny. You're being a dark horse. What games are you and Ulick up to?' She winked, with the eye farthest from Mrs Fly. A wink that explained whatever they were up to she understood and would support.

'I haven't heard from him any more,' said Virginia. 'There was no reason why I should have done.' Mrs Thompson looked deflated.

'Well, I expect he'll follow up the meeting. They're so unpredictable, these days, the young. That's their trouble.'

Already Mrs Fly was beginning to sense that she and Mrs Thompson were getting on quite extraordinarily well. They understood each other. They felt the same. In appreciation of these feelings Mrs Fly's blood rose in temperature – she could feel it like an incoming tide – all round her body, and her normally ashy cheeks slowly changed to the colour of a foggy plum. Hands shaking a little, she offered Mrs Thompson a cigarette. The tips of her fingers were quite red. She lowered her voice a little: she had been conscious of it rising since Mrs Thompson's arrival.

'The thing about Ginny is, she never *exerts* herself, do

you Ginny? She never *puts herself over*, if you know what I
mean.'

With a slight incline of her head which in no way indic-
ated that she was taking sides against Virginia, Mrs
Thompson conveyed that she knew very well what Mrs
Fly meant.

An hour later they were calling each other Ruth and
Rita, and Virginia was still listening. To break the
monotony, she got up and poured them small glasses of
medium-dry sherry.

'Ah,' exclaimed Mrs Thompson, 'the very brand Ulick
always buys me when I turn down the offer of a gin.' She
drank the whole glass in one. This degree of sophistication
unnerved Mrs Fly who, as usual, was pecking at her drink
with ridiculous little sips. Not to be outdone, she sipped a
little faster.

Virginia, predicting that the subject of Ulick Brand
would now be dwelt upon once more, decided to leave.
Ulick's house, tree, piano, dressing-room, face, gold cuff-
links and crinkly smile had all been on her mind too much
lately. She had tried to banish the thoughts, but they had
persisted. Last night she had dreamt of him. They had
played a duet on his piano together, kissing at the end of
every bar. Still, now, at midday, she could remember his
lips on hers. She had no wish to hear him discussed again.
Quietly she left the room and went upstairs to fetch her
purse. A wicked plan had come to her which would, perhaps, add a little spice to the tedious day.

When she arrived back at lunch time half the bottle of
sherry had gone. Her mother and Mrs Thompson were in
the kitchen, Mrs Fly draining the peas, Mrs Thompson
sitting at the table smoking, chipping her ash on to the
floor – a habit which, in the majority of people, Mrs Fly
could not abide.

Virginia unwrapped her parcel.

'I've bought a bottle,' she said, gaily, 'to celebrate.' She put a bottle of Mateus Rosé on the table.

'Ooh!' Her mother gave a little whoop. 'My favourite. How kind of you, dear.'

Mrs Thompson fingered the label on the bottle. 'I suppose, Rita, that with your life, you enjoy a little glass of wine for lunch every day?'

Mrs Thompson hesitated.

'Well, sometimes I do and I sometimes don't,' she admitted. 'Depends. Of course, in the old days, with Bill, we'd crack half a bottle of champagne every Sunday morning at eleven o'clock.'

'Really?' This time Mrs Fly was suitably impressed.

At lunch, Virginia had one glass of wine. The others had several. But still a quarter of the bottle remained. Mrs Fly suggested they should finish it with their coffee.

By this time both she and Mrs Thompson were in good spirits. They drew chairs up into the french windows in the sitting-room, and opened them. A warm breeze came into the room. The sky was cloudless, grey-blue; the Surrey hillocks turning to light spring green – but still depressing, Virginia thought.

'Lovely, lovely, lovely,' said Mrs Thompson, plumping herself down into an armchair. 'The softness of the air – it reminds me of Monte Carlo.'

If Mrs Fly felt that her new friend might be exaggerating, she did not show it.

'Of course,' she said, as the two things connected in her mind, 'you must have been a débutante.'

Mrs Thompson smiled widely, her eyes very bright.

'Well,' she said, 'in those days, you know, débutantes *were* débutantes.'

'Indeed they were!' Mrs Fly clapped her hands, but the clap went wrong. The fingers of one hand slipped into the palm of the other, scarcely making a noise. 'Why, I remember I used to cut out pictures of all the beautiful girls in their ostrich feathers going to be presented.'

'Ostrich feathers, such ostrich feathers,' murmured Mrs Thompson. She stretched out her legs in front of her. Her stockings puckered over her knees.

Virginia broke the nostalgic silence.

'Mrs Thompson used to have tea at the Ritz,' she said to her mother.

'The Ritz Piccadilly?' Mrs Fly felt another rush of warm blood round her body, and was grateful for the breeze. Funny, she thought, how sometimes words just slid out all in one, before you had time to divide them up.

Mrs Thompson managed a modest voice.

'Well, you know, the Ritz was *the* place to have tea. Always has been. I loved the Ritz. I loved theatre-going, too. Going to theatres. All the velvets, all the buttonholes. And supper afterwards somewhere you could dance.'

'The Savoy?' Mrs Fly had read about dancing at the Savoy, and the question was nice and short.

'Places like that,' said Mrs Thompson. She stared down the length of undernourished lawn, her eyes glazed with remembrance of those glamorous days. 'And then my escort would escort me home,' (she pronounced both words the same), 'and we'd have a small drink and turn on the gramophone.' She paused, then added: 'Ah, the things I could tell you.'

Mrs Fly pressed her a little.

'You mean you had your own flat?'

'I had my own flat.'

'That means you must have been very well off.' Mrs Thompson considered. Then she said:

'I managed to support myself in fine style, I will admit.'

The breeze was so soft, her face so warm, her mind so

plastic, at that moment it would have been easy to admit anything.

'But I thought débutantes in those days didn't work?' Mrs Fly, pouring the last of the Mateus Rosé into her own glass, was confused.

'Ah.'

'What did you work at?' Mrs Fly persisted.

'Ah.' Again Mrs Thompson paused. 'I suppose you could have called me an entertainer.'

'*Show business?* I've always longed to know someone in show business. It must be such a world apart, I've always thought.' Mrs Fly felt her eyelids drifting downwards. She snapped them up. 'Stage door Johnnies,' she said. 'You must have been besieged by stage door Johnnies.'

'There were men interested,' agreed Mrs Thompson.

'And you let them come back to your flat? You must have been very before-your-time.' A mixture of shock and awe in Mrs Fly's voice. Mrs Thompson drained her glass. She could never remember feeling like this on gin. It was all according to what you were used to, she supposed.

'My dear Ruth. In my line of business, escorts have been escorting pretty young girls back to their flats for thousands of years.'

There. She had said it. After all these years of silence, it had slipped out. She turned to Mrs Fly, waiting to be struck, to be turned out of the house. But at the same time an immeasurable weight rolled away from her: her limbs, her mind felt lighter. She wanted to laugh. She wanted to cry, to dance, to sing, to shout out loud: *Forgive me, Bill.*

But it was Mrs Fly who began to giggle.

'Oh, you'll be the death of me, Rita! No wonder my mother disapproved of débutantes! Presented at Court then giving the chaperon the slip – such carryings on.' She rocked back and forth in her arm chair. 'You'll be telling me next you – let them make advances!' Then suddenly she was quiet. 'To think what I missed,' she said. 'Ted came to tea every Sunday and we were only allowed to walk to church and back alone. He was the only man who ever courted me.'

'What you missed, dear.' Mrs Thompson let the giggles burst forth now. The irony of the situation was too much for her. 'What you missed! The stories I could tell . . . You'd never believe.'

Both women squirmed in their seats with laughter, their hands sprawling over the wide chair arms, their legs sliding apart to reveal wedges of white thigh above stocking tops. Tears spurted from their cloudy eyes.

'Oh, dear me.'

'Oh, deary, deary me.'

Virginia crept away. They didn't notice her going, or hear her laughter. Upstairs, she took out her diary. She wrote in it spasmodically, only noting things she thought worth recording. Nothing sad, or to do with herself. *To-day, unbeknown to her, my mother befriended an old tart*, she wrote. And then she felt foolish, laughing out loud to herself, and the joke, as is often the nature of unshared jokes, began to pall.

Mr Fly arrived home, as he promised, punctually at four. He unloaded his lawn mower into the garage slowly. If he timed things right he'd only have to be with the two of them for twenty minutes before setting off for the station again.

In spite of the breeze, the afternoon was muggy, the sky had turned quite grey. After the long drive Mr Fly was sweaty and tired. Thirsty. Mrs Thompson or not, he wanted his tea.

He went to the kitchen, washed his hands and patted his neck with water. It seemed to him that the place wasn't its usual tidy self. But then he remembered and understood. His wife would naturally want to leave the washing up till Mrs Thompson had gone.

He went to the dining-room – it was always dining-room tea for visitors. But there, a far from average sight met his eyes. The table was still covered with congealed plates from lunch: chairs askew, nothing stacked, a nasty smell of cold vegetables.

Worried, now, Mr Fly ran to the sitting-room.

A few moments later Virginia heard him calling. She ran downstairs.

'Ginny – whatever . . .?'

'What are they doing?'

'Asleep. I can't wake them.'

They went to the sitting-room. It was getting dark. The two women, both with their mouths open, slept in their separate chairs. On the floor lay the upturned bottle of wine, and a few cigarette stubs that had fallen from the ash tray.

'A most unusual sight,' said Mr Fly. He put his arm round his daughter.

'They're friends for life,' Virginia giggled.

'Heaven forbid, Ginny.'

'Well, at least I won't have her after me any more.'

'Nor you will – So untidy,' he added, turning away from the scene.

They went to the kitchen. Virginia put on the kettle, fetched scones from the larder, strawberry jam and cream, which Mrs Fly considered bad for her husband and would not allow. Mr Fly watched his daughter, happily, rubbing together his hands.

'We'd better let them sleep it off. Better not be there when they wake up, either. Funny, your mother, like this, you know. You wouldn't call her even an average drinker, would you? She hardly touches a drop. Perhaps that Mrs

Thompson is a bad influence, though she seemed a nice enough woman. Perhaps she has a dark past.'

'She has,' said Virginia. This made Mr Fly laugh. His daughter had a fine sense of humour. Must have got it from him. He stretched out a hand towards her.

'Selfish though it may be, Ginny,' he said, 'I'm glad you're here.'

Chapter 8

Mrs Thompson spent the night with the Flys. After a peaceful supper Virginia and her father, peeping round the kitchen door, had watched Mrs Fly and her friend negotiate the stairs in some confusion, still giving the odd weak giggle, and leaning upon one another for support.

The next morning, for the first time for years, Virginia was up before her mother and cooked her father's breakfast. He went off to work with a happy wink.

'She's not going to be able to get at me for a while, now, is she? After *this*. Tell her I recommend a raw egg mixed with milk and aspirin.'

As soon as he had gone, the telephone rang. Virginia answered it in the hall. She was unaccustomed to telephone conversations. She found them nerve-racking.

'Virginia Fly?'

'Yes?' At the sound of a strange man's voice her heart beat faster.

'This is Ulick Brand. I thought I was bound to get on to your mother.'

'Oh, Ulick – Mr Brand. She's in bed.'

'I'm sorry to hear that. Ill, you mean?'

'No, no. She – you remember Mrs Thompson?'

'Indeed.'

'She came here yesterday and I think there must have been something in their sherry. Mrs Thompson had to spend the night. She's not awake yet, either.' Ulick laughed.

'I can hardly hear you,' he said.

'I don't want to wake them up.'

'Quite.' He paused. 'I wondered if you were free to-night?' Virginia wondered if he could hear her heart. She traced a pencil round the picture on the telephone message book: an icy mountain rising into a brilliant blue sky, and reflecting into an equally unlikely lake.

'It's almost the end of the holidays,' she said at last.

'Does that stop you being free?'

'Not really.'

'Would you like to see a film and have dinner?'

'Yes, I would. Thank you,' she added. The mountain multiplied into four, with four reflections.

'Because funnily enough,' Ulick was saying, 'I have some business to do, God help me, in Guildford on Tuesday morning. So if you like to spend the night in my dressing-room again, you could cook me breakfast and I'd drive you back. What do you think of that as a plan?'

'Fine,' said Virginia. 'How did you get my number?'

'Simple detective work. Come to the house at about seven-thirty, then, O.K.? And don't dress up. An old pair of trousers'll do. See you. 'Bye.'

He was gone before Virginia had time to say good-bye. She sat quite still for a few moments, still tracing the mountain, which had gone back to one now. She noticed the handle of the receiver glistened with sweat. She rubbed it on her skirt.

'Who was that?' Mrs Fly stood at the top of the stairs in a candlewick dressing-gown. Her hair was flattened by a net, her grey face creased and the whites of her screwed-up eyes the colour of spring rhubarb. She had remembered to wipe off the greasy surface of her lipstick, but the stain beneath remained, an unhealthy purple.

'Oh, a friend. For me.'

Mrs Fly tightened the belt of her dressing-gown. She began to come down the stairs, slowly, holding the banisters.

'My poor head,' she said. 'I don't know what came over me. There must have been something in that wine you bought, Ginny. I've never been taken like that in my life before. Are you all right?'

'Absolutely, thank you.'

'Well, I don't know. And Rita was in a very poor way last night. I'd better get her a cup of tea. I wouldn't be surprised if she'd like to stay here for the day and recover. I shall go down to the wine merchant myself, later, and ask him. It oughtn't to be allowed.' She went into the kitchen. 'You got your father's breakfast?'

'And dinner and tea.'

'I hope you didn't let him overdo it, the jam and what-not.'

Virginia followed her into the kitchen. The small tight line of Mrs Fly's mouth indicated that she had no intention of thanking her daughter for her help.

'I'm going to London in an hour,' said Virginia. 'I'll be away to-night and back to-morrow morning.'

Mrs Fly stopped the tap, leaving the kettle half-filled. 'But it's almost term-time.'

'So?'

'Haven't you all that preparation to do?'

'No.'

'Well, it's not up to me. You're over twenty-one. Don't overdo it, late nights, that's all I say. It's only fair to the school to be fit for the term.' Her hand shook a little on the tea caddy. 'I think I'll make a nice bacon and egg pie for Rita's lunch.' She knew that was Virginia's favourite thing. 'Sure you don't want to stay?'

'Sure, thank you.'

'You're after more chop-suey, no doubt?' She gave an understanding smile. Virginia looked infuriated. Sometimes, Mrs Fly thought, she could never get through to the girl. Oh well, better change the subject. 'What a head,' she said again.

'Father said to tell you aspirin mixed with raw egg and milk might help.'

'Did he just?' Mrs Fly banged a couple of cups on to the table. The thud made her wince. 'Wait till something's poisoned him and see what cure *I* recommend! Now, where did you hide the sugar?' She screwed up her eyes again to avoid the hurting sun. Virginia took the sugar bowl from its normal place, wished her mother a quick recovery and a happy day with Mrs Thompson, and left for London.

She took a taxi from Waterloo to the King's Road. There, she was determined to spend the £15 she had brought with her. The shops were overflowing with brilliant clothes. She trembled in and out of silks and satins and velvets, all quite unlike anything she had ever considered buying before, and came out into the sun again, with nothing, trying to make up her mind. Mrs Thompson's advice, given unasked for, was loud in her head.

'*Allure*, dear, is what you want to think of. All your greys – who wants to be demure? Of course, my age, I'm past fancy dressing. But in the old days I'd slay them with the softness of my clothes, velvets and satins and so on.' She winked. 'Make a man feel he wants to *stroke* you, that's what you want to do, and you're half way there.' Gazing into the distance, she gave a small shudder, then dragged her eyes back to Virginia. 'With a little know-how, Ginny,' she said, 'you could have the boys trailing after you. If I had your figure – even now . . .' She allowed herself a small, nostalgic sigh.

Finally, half visualising a queue of men behind her, Virginia settled for a pair of purple velvet trousers, which emphasised the thinness of her legs, and a gypsy-like top, covered with extravagant embroidery, that the assistant said would look better without a bra.

It was nice, walking along with her bags, money all gone, to feel that Ulick's house was so near. She resisted the temptation to walk down his street.

But there were several hours until she was due. On a sudden inspiration she went to a call box, looked up Caroline's married name, and rang her. They hadn't seen each other for six years but she was the only person, apart from the professor, Virginia knew in London.

'Caroline?' Virginia found herself peculiarly nervous now the telephone had been answered.

'Yes? Speaking.'

'It's Virginia. Virginia Fly.'

'*Virginia!* God, it's been years.'

'I was just in London for the day. I hope you don't mind my ringing . . .'

'Of course not,' Caroline butted in. She sounded busy.

'I'm going out to-night and I just wondered if I could possibly drop in for a cup of tea and change in your house?' Virginia paused. 'It would be so nice to see you again.'

'Of course, what a heavenly idea. But I'm afraid I'm *just* on my way out. In fact you were lucky to have caught me.' She listed all the places she was going to, convincingly. But she sounded quite kind, friendly. 'But I tell you what, the au pair's here. Come round when you feel like it, make yourself at home, and I'll try to get back before you leave.'

'Are you sure?' Virginia was really unnerved now, but she had nowhere else to go. 'Thank you very much.'

'Don't be *ridiculous*,' Caroline babbled on. 'I only wish you'd given me some notice then we could have had lunch or something. There's so much to catch up on.' She paused. Then: 'Just tell me, are you nearly married or anything?'

'Well,' said Virginia. 'Not exactly.'

'You mean something's in the air?'

'You could put it like that.'

'I should hope so, after all these years.' Caroline laughed, nicely. 'You will let me know, won't you? I must rush. If I miss you, do ring again.'

When she had put the telephone down Virginia took a Biro from her bag. She couldn't resist trying out the name. On the cover of one of the telephone books she wrote it: *Mrs Ulick Brand.*

Caroline Summers lived in a small house off the Cromwell Road. The au pair girl let Virginia in, showed her the kitchen, and went out. Virginia was left to explore.

It wasn't that she felt in any way inquisitive: she simply wanted to know what a house belonging to a young married couple was like, to imagine how it would feel to own it. She started in the kitchen, a pine room still warm with the smell of cooked lunch. The huge fridge was full. It included a large cut-glass bowl of fruit salad elaborately decorated with cream: for visitors to-night, perhaps. Dinner parties. Virginia wondered about married people's dinner parties in this sort of house. A hired help for the evening, probably. Michael fussing about the drinks, Caroline introducing people with great ease, and getting them to talk. Virginia wondered if she would be able to cope with all that.

On a blackboard on the wall Caroline had scrawled messages to herself: *Remember! 12 yogurts, 1 lb. cooking cheese, get M's lighter mended.* The last reminder filled Virginia with something like jealousy: it would be nice to have someone wanting you to get their lighter mended, someone relying on you for small things as well as large.

She went to the sitting-room. There were signs of Caroline's hurried departure: newspapers on the floor, a cushion about to slide from the sofa. Automatically Virginia plumped it up. There was a predictable table full of drinks, almost identical to Ulick's, and a large untidy desk bearing traces of both Michael and Caroline: their things all muddled up together. Virginia read a note, perhaps written last night: *Darling, if you get in before me will you start on Lucy's story as I promised her? All love C.*

In the main bedroom she found a pair of braces on Caroline's dressing-table, and a crowd of framed photographs: Michael and Caroline on their wedding day, as she remembered them, both fatter in the face then, smiling outside a country church near Andover; Caroline with her first child, a christening picture; Michael out of focus on a boat, obviously taken by his wife: a two-year-old boy sitting on a rug with bricks; Caroline at some sort of première with Michael, leaning on his arm, very elegant, but harder and thinner than Virginia recalled.

She sat at the stool, fingered the silver brushes, and made up her mind. If Ulick Brand asked her to marry him, she would say yes.

Some hours later, having used Caroline's bath, powder and scent, and having brushed her hair with the silver brush (and left it loose), she put on her new clothes, admired herself – almost unrecognisable, wasn't she? – in a long mirror, left the house and took a taxi to Chelsea. Her hands were shaking.

Ulick opened the door. For a moment he didn't recognise her. Then:

'Virginia, you look terrific,' he said, kissing her on both cheeks. 'I knew you could.' Virginia said nothing, but blushed. 'No need to blush. I mean it.' He took her hand and led her upstairs. The drawing-room looked pretty in the evening light. It smelt faintly of polish and flowers.

In the middle of the room Ulick turned to face Virginia. 'Is the transformation all for me?' he asked, laughing.

'Who else?' Virginia said, shyly. Then, more daring: 'If you don't mind my saying, you look very nice too.' He wore a beautiful flowered silk shirt, and his face was more handsome than she remembered.

He didn't seem to notice the remark but was at the drinks table mixing things. Virginia wondered if the action was automatic in his world: people arrive – give them an instant drink. At home, the average guest had to sit it out for several hours before he was offered anything stronger than coffee or tea.

'I've had the most bloody awful lunch,' he said, 'it put me off work for the whole afternoon. Rows, rows, rows. God I hate rows. They upset my stomach. Give me indigestion. Do you ever have rows with anyone?'

'No. Only silences, with my mother, sometimes.'

'Better than rows. Anyhow, they're over for to-day. We'll go out and have a smashing evening.'

He smiled, and gave her one of the thick glasses of whisky: she liked the glass better to-night. More used to it, it didn't hurt her hand.

She sat back in a sofa of silk cushions, one foot under her, one resting on the thick carpet, and felt a sense of infinite peace. She could sit here evening after evening, listening to him, understanding about his office rows (for she presumed what he had been referring to were office rows), soothing him, pouring his drinks, offering comfort.

'You look very serious,' said Ulick. 'What are you thinking?'

'About your life.'

'Oh, my life. That's something I try not to think about in the round, as it were. I try to stick to thinking only about each day as it comes. It's an old philosophy, but it works quite well when you get used to it.' It may have

147

been Virginia's imagination, but for a moment she thought he looked quite sad.

They went to a lively film about Tchaikovsky. Halfway through, Ulick took one of Virginia's hands, traced round the shape of her nails with his finger, then put it back again. The gesture, she found, made her breathe very fast. She hoped he wouldn't notice. Later they went to dinner in a small Polish restaurant in Battersea. The chef, a huge laughing man, joined them at their table for most of the evening, pressing bottles of free wine upon them and entertaining them with stories of his childhood in Poland. Back in the car Ulick put his hand on Virginia's knee, and she just stopped herself from telling him that it made her feel quite extraordinarily unusual.

In the house, he led her at once up to his brown felt dressing-room. There, he put his arms round her.

'Will you kiss me?' he said.

'I don't think I ought to,' Virginia replied automatically. Her body stiffened.

'Why not?'

'I can't really think.'

Ulick kissed her for a while. Then he stood back.

'I've been wanting to do that all the evening. You're irresistible.' Virginia smiled. He picked up her small suitcase and led the way to his room. Virginia followed.

This, too, was a dark room: navy hessian on the walls, lights that shone dim blobs of light on to the carpet.

'Get into bed,' said Ulick, putting down her case. 'I'll join you in a moment.' He disappeared through an almost invisible door in the wall to the bathroom.

Virginia got undressed, folded up her clothes neatly, through years of habit, and got into bed naked. She wondered vaguely if, when Ulick came back, she should go to the bathroom and do her teeth. Ulick's sheets were very expensive; cool and smooth even after a few nights wear.

Virginia wiggled about in the huge bed with pleasure, stretching her toes down to the coolest bits, fanning her arms across the pillows. Very much later, it seemed, Ulick came back, a towel wrapped round his waist.

'Move over.' Virginia giggled, shutting her eyes. Ulick got into bed and switched off the light. In a moment he was kissing her again, more fiercely this time, and she could feel the whole length of his body pressed against the whole length of hers. His hand ran over her breast, stomach, thigh, causing her to tremble.

'You're shaking,' he said.

'I can't help it.'

'Aren't you used to this sort of thing?'

'No.'

'Good.' He lifted her head on to his shoulder, very gently, and touched her hair and her eyelids.

'Shall I tell you something?' Virginia felt reckless.

'What? Anything. Tell me anything you like.'

'I've never felt like this in my life before, never, ever, ever, ever.'

'Haven't you?'

'I couldn't stop thinking about your wisteria tree, and wondering what you were doing.'

'Well, I thought about you quite a bit, too. I thought: she's not my usual kind of girl, but there's something about her. Those awful gloves!' Virginia giggled again, and rubbed her nose against his face. 'I thought: perhaps I'd better see her again just to make sure she's *not* my kind of girl. Then you arrived looking so pretty, and you laughed at my jokes and didn't ask awkward questions.'

'So?'

'So here we are.'

'And?'

'And I hope we will be again, lots of times.'

Ulick crushed her to him, forcing her body to go slack and her legs to part. She screwed up her eyes against his throat, so that her mind became a screen of black dots on blackness. Then, with a shocking suddenness, the scene lighted. The black dots turned to yellow. Light flooded from somewhere. She felt Ulick go rigid and push her away. She opened her eyes.

The bedroom was in full light. A woman stood by he door, quivering. She was tall, with curly hair and a tragic face, about thirty. She might have been crying.

'What's this woman doing in *our* bed?' she asked, looking at Virginia. Ulick held the sheet in both hands under his chin. The whites of his knuckles showed. He blinked very calmly.

'What are you doing here?'

'It's *our* house, you may remember. Our bed. I have my keys. You're my husband.' She didn't move.

'Curious timing for a visit,' said Ulick.

'I have every right to come here whenever I like. Unless you buy me out.' Her voice was very low and quiet. She moved over to the bed, and stood looking down at Ulick and Virginia. 'I'm sorry to interrupt,' she said, 'but could this woman go now?'

'No,' said Ulick. 'It's you who must go.'

'Never,' said the woman. She sounded tired. She sat on the bed. Ulick moved his legs. 'Remember, darling, what you always said?' She smiled very slightly. 'You always said – we always joked – that if ever I caught you at it, I wasn't to go. I was to wait around until you got rid of the – woman.'

'Those were our joking days,' said Ulick. 'You seem to have forgotten, they're over now.'

The woman took a cigarette and lighter out of her bag. She reached over to the bedside table for the ashtray, which she balanced on Ulick's knee as if she had done the same thing many times before. She puffed smoke into the air, very calmly, as if this were a normal situation. Her eyes were bright green, strained. Very slowly she swivelled her head towards Virginia.

'What's your name?' she asked.

'Don't say,' replied Ulick quickly. 'Don't say anything to her.' Virginia saw the woman flinch.

'Well,' she said, through more smoke, so it was impossible to see the effort on her face that sounded in her voice, 'we seem to have come to an impasse, then, don't we? Because I'm not leaving.'

'You are,' said Ulick. 'Please go quietly with no fuss. I'll ring you in the morning.'

'No,' said the woman.

There was a long silence. Then Virginia, who felt her body and mind numb and stiff with shock, heard her own voice a long way off speaking some kind of common sense.

'This is ridiculous. I'll go,' she said. The woman laughed.

'It's quite amusing, if you think about it,' she said. Ulick put an arm over Virginia's chest, restraining her.

'Don't move. Imogen will go.' So that was her name. Mrs Imogen Brand.

'I won't,' said Imogen.

'But I definitely will.' Virginia kicked at the bed clothes, baring her breasts. 'I don't want to come between you.'

'Quite,' said Imogen, staring at Virginia's nipples. 'You see, darling, your woman's more sensible than you.' She patted Ulick's knee. His eyes froze.

'This is a ludicrous and undignified scene,' he said. 'If you persist in being so obstinate, please go away for a few minutes so that Virginia can get dressed and I can talk to her.'

Imogen stubbed out her cigarette and stood up.

'Very well. I'll do that.' She left the room, very tall and straight, conscious of the beauty of her movements.

As soon as she had gone Virginia sprang up and began to dress fast. Ulick sat on the edge of the bed, his head in his hands.

'I'm sorry,' he said. 'What can I say?'

'It doesn't matter.'

'I should have told you I was married.'

'It wasn't relevant to our situation.'

'That's true. She's never done anything like this before. Though she was so impossible at lunch to-day, I thought something was up.' He looked up at Virginia. 'Stay the night in the dressing-room and we can talk it all over in the morning.'

'No thank you, really.' She combed her hair with her fingers.

'Where will you go?'

'I have friends.' Ulick nodded.

'All right for money?'

'Plenty.'

'It was such a nice evening, too. I always forget to remember that things get snatched away.'

Virginia smiled at him.

'Don't be over dramatic, or think any more about it. I was just an easy lay, except there wasn't quite time to get laid. Things are all a matter of timing.'

'It wasn't like that at all. Don't think of it like that. I *like* you. You *listened* to me.'

'Most plain girls are good listeners.' She picked up her case. 'Well, I'll be going.' Ulick, too, stood up.

'I'm sorry,' he said, again. 'Can I call you?'

'I don't think there's much point,' Virginia said. 'In fact, I'd really rather you didn't. Please don't. It wouldn't be good for my fantasy world.' She managed another smile.

'O.K.' He stood up and kissed her on the cheek. They were both limp, drained, now, all desire gone. 'Good-bye, Virginia Fly. Be careful who you marry.'

At the door of the room Virginia met Imogen, who had changed into a white cotton dressing-gown that showed the lines of her breasts, and thighs.

'That was quick,' she said. 'I'll show you out.' Virginia followed her down the stairs. 'You must understand, Ulick and I have a perfectly dreadful married life,' she was saying, 'but we can never quite get round to giving it up. Habit or something, I suppose, though now I've moved out maybe we'll get down to it. Anyhow, I hope you won't have been too affected by all this – or too charmed. He's a real old charmer when he wants to be, isn't he? Bloody awful for most of the time, though.' She opened the door, her eyes sparkling and hard. 'I'll tell you what, though. I'm a well-known dog-in-the-manger. I don't want him half the time, but I don't want anyone else to have him either. So I should leave him alone, if I were you. Unless, that is, you want to find yourself cited.' She smiled, witchlike, in the gloomy light from the street. Virginia straightened herself: still she only came to Imogen's shoulder.

'You'll find a taxi in the King's Road.' Imogen pointed a long white hand in the right direction. 'You must admit, it was quite funny,' she added. 'One day, perhaps, I'll tell you the real story of our marriage.'

'Thank you,' said Virginia, 'but I wouldn't be terribly interested. Neither you, nor Ulick, nor your marriage concerns me in any way. Now I must go.' At the bottom of the steps she looked up to find Imogen still watching her. She decided to take a parting shot, for all its childishness. 'The bed will still be warm,' she shouted.

The door slammed. Virginia ran.

In a telephone box in the King's Road the tears came. Choking sobs she was incapable of controlling. She stood for some time, leaning her head against the glass panes of the box, waiting for the spasms that wracked her body to die away. It was cold and the air was a ball of stale smoke.

When she had calmed down she picked up a telephone book and dialled the professor's number. She could stay the night there – he had often suggested it – and go home by train in the morning. The telephone rang eleven times.

'Is that the Professor?'

'Who is it, for heaven's sake? My God, Virginia Fly.'

'Yes.'

'Why? It's two o'clock, isn't it? In the morning.'

'I expect so. I'm sorry to bother you so late – '

' – that's no trouble.'

' – but can I come over and spend the rest of the night? There've been a few complications.'

'Complications? My dear Virginia, of course. Forgive me if I sound so stupid with sleep. Put yourself in a taxi at once. I am waiting for you.'

In the taxi Virginia felt weak with exhaustion. She lay back on the leather ridged seat that was still warm from the previous passenger. Perhaps that would be a good wholetime function in life, she thought. Warming things for other people.

'Virginia Fly, whatever is it about you?' she asked out loud.

The professor was dressed; the lights were on. He had made up a bed on the huge sofa and had a glass of brandy waiting.

'What delicious clothes,' he said, when he saw her anguished face. 'But you must go to sleep quickly because

154

you look quite tired. I won't disturb you in the morning, and the sun can't get through the thickness of the curtains. So sleep on, and then we will have a breakfast.'

The brandy warmed Virginia, stopped her shivering. She watched the professor, his shadowy hulk by the desk, shuffling through papers.

'Now, is there anything I can get for you?' Virginia knew he was trying not to look concerned.

'Nothing. And thank you for being so kind.'

'Don't be so foolish.' A little later he left her.

The sofa was very comfortable. In the dark, the evening ran through Virginia's mind like a film. At one point, there were words, sub-titles, upon the screen: *Try not to think of your life in the round. Think only of to-day.*

When she thought about it, Ulick was pretty unoriginal.

Virginia felt quite happy before she went to sleep.

She was woken by the professor drawing back the curtains, letting in broad shafts of late spring sun through the vast windows. They lit up the warm shambles of the room.

'I have croissants for us,' he said. 'They do very good croissants down the road, fresh every morning, and you can't tell me you're not hungry?'

He went away and came back with a tray laid with pretty china: black cherry jam to go with the croissants. He set it on a low table beside the sofa and drew up a chair.

'It is so long since I shared breakfast with anyone, I am quite out of practice.' He was factual rather than self-pitying. Virginia praised the Austrian coffee. 'There are some things we can do,' he said, smiling.

No sooner had he buttered his croissant than he got up, crossed the room to the fireplace and fetched the photograph of his wife and daughter. He handed it to Virginia. The family at breakfast, she thought. This time, she was ready for it.

'That is my wife and daughter in the Alps.' He tapped the photograph with three fingers. 'They were killed soon after that picture was taken. I loved them very much. I still love them, but they are dead. Oh, my God, I can't make a speech – Virginia Fly, will you marry me?'

Virginia looked up at him, handed back the photograph. Backlit by the sun, his grey hair stood up like a spiky halo. His shoulders were hunched forward, his kind eyes tense, as he waited for her answer.

'I meant to wait till after breakfast,' he added, 'but seeing you this morning, asleep, I couldn't.'

Virginia smiled. Then she lay back on her pillows, shutting her eyes. The screen beneath her lids still glowed with sun. Childish incidents, silly speculations, grown-up longings, all from the past, came to her mind. She compared them with the present.

The professor, sitting beside her in silence, waited.

Chapter 9

Virginia and Caroline had talked about marriage long before they ever discussed sex. Aged nine, Caroline was determined to marry a millionaire. Virginia was quite happy with the thought of a farmer.

One summer holidays Caroline was staying with the Flys for a week, sharing the spare-room with Virginia. Lights were out: they were supposed to be trying to go to sleep.

'He'll propose to me on a yacht,' Caroline was saying, 'somewhere in the Mediterranean.'

'Very ordinary,' scoffed Virginia. 'Me, I'll be on a walking tour in Northumberland. It'll suddenly come on to rain very hard and I'll shelter in a nearby barn. I'll just be sitting on the hay waiting for it to stop, when this lovely farmer comes in. He asks me if I'd like to come into the farmhouse to get warm and dry and have something to eat. So we go and sit in front of his fire and *straight away* he says he loves me terribly much and will I marry him? Of course I say yes, and we live happily ever after.'

Half asleep, she imagined the exquisite pleasure of baking bread for her farmer, sitting by his side in the evenings, feeding his hens, calling him across the farmyard, raising his children. For years this daydream stuck with her but, somehow, she never went on a walking tour in Northumberland.

When Virginia was twenty, the girl next door, who for many years had been noted and pitied for her lack of looks, married a sailor.

'And if *she* can get someone, then anyone can,' Virginia remembered her mother saying, as they walked back from the church. The bride, looking her worst in a lot of misguided make-up, had just driven off in a hired Rolls. 'Still, I suppose you must admit it, she looks pretty radiant.'

At that moment, Virginia, at twenty, would have done anything to swop places with her plain neighbour. The sailor may not have been the most eligible of men, but at least he was a husband.

The next wedding to reduce Virginia's spirits was Caroline's. That was a very grand, happy, affair: trembly prayers and the Wedding March, tear-jerking in its optimism, in a small Norman church in Hampshire. Later, hundreds of painted people squashed into a marquee that smelt sickly with gardenias; Caroline, laughing all the time, loving every moment of it.

In a way, Virginia was pleased for Caroline. She seemed to be genuinely happy. Certainly she could describe real love. Those were the days when she still told Virginia everything.

'It's an *all over* feeling,' she said. 'When Michael's not there, then half of me is not there either. He makes me dizzy when he comes into the room, physically dizzy. And sometimes, when I'm trying to be sensible, I find myself being quite stupid because I can't concentrate on anything except for the fact that I love him so much. I'd do anything in the world for him. Anything. He's the whole point of my existence. Everything's tolerable, now, just because he's alive.'

'Look at the increasing divorce rate,' said Virginia, who'd never felt physically dizzy at the thought of Charlie or anyone else. 'No doubt all those people who are divorced now said much the same sort of thing in the beginning.'

'Ah, but with us it's different.' Caroline was confident in the cliché. Her confidence irritated Virginia.

'That's what they all say,' she said.

But in Caroline's case it really did seem to be different, judging from the signs in her house, and the few occasions on which Virginia now talked to her. She seemed to be happy. She seemed to have a thriving married life.

As far as Virginia was concerned, her marriage soon meant the beginning of the end of their close friendship. For a while, they kept up communications. Caroline treated Virginia to funny and explicit descriptions of childbirth. She even disclosed secrets of married sex – 'it becomes plainer,' she said. But within a couple of years Caroline's husband, children, house and life took up all her time. Virginia rarely came to London and when she did, and they met, they found they had little left in common. Caroline was full of domestic chatter that bored Virginia, and there was nothing in Virginia's life that aroused Caroline's interest. And so, by mutual, unspoken consent, they faded from each other's lives. Christmas cards, holiday postcards, an annual birthday present for the eldest child – Virginia's godchild – was all that was left. Virginia regretted the passing of their friendship. It was the only satisfactory one she had ever had. Still, she felt it had been good enough to stand being renewed at some auspicious moment. When she married herself, perhaps. Then, if the fibres had not frayed too far, they could carry on where they had left off. They would be back on the same plane again, re-bound together by the fact that they both had husbands, families, and all the problems of married life which go a long way in bringing the most disparate women together.

It was soon after the birth of Caroline's first child – an event which had a depressing effect on Virginia – that she began to pin her marital hopes on Charlie Oakhampton Jr. She began to detect, between the emerald lines of his letters, a certain optimism for the future. Surely it wasn't without design that he wrote in so detailed a way descriptions of his house, the American countryside, his mother, and his weekends watching baseball? If he intended Virginia to become familiar with the minutae of his life, he succeeded. And gradually it came to her, with some effort of will, that it might be quite a good sort of life – far from the idyllic British life with a comfortable, unassuming British husband that in optimistic moments she imagined might materialise one day – but an exciting change, and you could get used to anything. She liked the idea of the narrowness of American suburban life, the idea of an energetic community in which every contribution counted. She imagined herself *taking part*, organising, helping, being called upon. Eagerly, she conveyed her feelings to Charlie. He (strangely, she thought at the time) didn't seem too interested in her reactions. He merely supplied her with even more details. On those occasions Virginia felt that, for the unskilled, letter writing was a bad form of communication: she had failed to express herself in a manner that he could respond to, and would have to wait till his arrival to tell him.

From time to time her enthusiasm for this new imagined life became strangled with doubts. She would picture the loneliness, the pettiness, the feeling that, should she hate it all, there would be no escape. But, again with great mental effort, she managed to bury these doubts almost as soon as she had warning of them: and her dream of the modern kitchen with its window overlooking the station-wagon and the neighbour's fence, Charlie eating waffles, the stacked up *ice box* (already she had abandoned the word Frigidaire in her mind) became a comfort to live with. It was just a matter of waiting till Charlie came to fetch her, and they could go back to Utah and put the dream into practice.

One Easter holiday the school arranged that Virginia's class, and the class above, should go to Switzerland – very reduced rates for fourteen nights, travel by coach. She and Mr Bluett were to be in charge.

Virginia found Switzerland an unsatisfactory, predictable country. The views, though magnificent, were unsurprising; for all their size, the mountains were tame things with their toy chalets and handfuls of goats. There was none of the wildness she had been expecting, and hoping for. Nevertheless, the holiday was a success. She was alone in her disappointment. The children energetically enjoyed themselves and Mr Bluett observed that the English millionaires who retired to the Lake of Geneva must feel they were in the next best place to home.

One evening, high in the mountains, after supper, Virginia and Mr Bluett went for a walk along the narrow village street. They intended to stop at the local bar for a bedtime *Glühwein*, but it was still not dark and the air was soft and refreshing. They both felt like walking on.

The road, which quickly became rougher, led up the mountain, curving by the side of tall dark pine trees on one side, and a rocky precipice on the other. They walked for half an hour without speaking, and finally came to rest on a pile of tree trunks in a clearing. Before them the moon was rising in a charcoal sky. A mountain, its cap silvered with snow, glared across at them from the other side of the pass. Somewhere below Virginia could hear the dull chink of cowbells: a most melancholy sound, she thought.

Mr Bluett, who was as sensitive to cold as he was to heat, fumbled with the strings of his anorak at his neck.

'The point about all this, Virginia,' he said, suddenly,

'is that it should be shared with someone.' Virginia raised her eyebrows at him but probably, in the almost-dark, he didn't see. 'I think all good things should be shared.' He sniffed, and rubbed at his wavy hair with the back of his hand.

'I'm not against enjoying nature by myself,' said Virginia, feeling any reply would be inadequate. 'I would rather that than other people's observations.'

'Ah, my dear girl, you are young. You can never have been in love, never have shared an early morning on the sea with someone, or a sunset in the Highlands. If you had, you wouldn't feel like you do.' He banged at his pocket for cigarettes. 'In the old days, you know, not so many years ago, Derek and I would run a couple of miles every morning before breakfast. Gym shoes in the dew, skinny vests with numbers on them from our racing days. I was twenty-six, I remember. Derek was nineteen. Our lucky numbers. We'd get back, a lather of sweat, shower down and take turns to make breakfast. Bacon and eggs. Then I was in trim for the day. A hundred vaults couldn't daunt me. In those days, I'd enjoy the whole day at school, lousy pupils or not, just thinking of the evening. You never came to our place, did you? We had a nice little cottage. Beams. You should come some time, though it's gone a bit to seed now Derek's left.' He let a shaft of smoke curl up over his face. 'He would have liked this, Derek. He liked moons over mountains and all that stuff. Oh well, there's no use getting morbid, is there? Had we better be on our way back?'

The confidences seemed to have exhausted him. They walked back to the village slowly, in silence again. Virginia, who had always imagined Mr Bluett to be a conventional bachelor living alone, re-organised her mind to this new picture of him with his ex-lover Derek. People were not in the habit of confiding in her: she felt flattered and full of understanding. Here was someone in a predicament every bit as sharp as her own, someone who was able to slap down feelings of self-pity as they surged upon him, and yet who was not able altogether to abandon remembrance of things past. It was admirable, the concealing of his loneliness: some people were good at disguise. Virginia condemned herself for never having guessed that beneath the cheerful exterior of her fellow teacher there lived a profoundly unhappy man.

Back at the chalet hotel – it was cold now and they were glad to return to its warmth and light – Virginia bought a bottle of wine which they drank in front of an open fire. They spoke of the school, their pupils, the staff, the events of this holiday. But just before they parted to go to bed, Mr Bluett, with some embarrassment this time, referred to their former conversation.

'Forgive me, Virginia,' he said, 'if earlier on I inflicted you with some of myself. I am not in favour of unburdening, but sometimes we are weak and cause our friends to suffer.' He gave a small, formal bow to cover his confusion, and was gone before Virginia could protest.

Later, in her small pine room, Virginia sat on the bed in the dark thinking of the middle-aged, homosexual gym master. Outside the open windows she could see a pair of almost identical mountains looming in the sky, dark shapes against darkness. She thought of Charlie – no, he wouldn't do. She couldn't pretend to herself. There was no one else to imagine.

'Damn you, Mr Bluett,' she said, out loud, lying back on the bed, still dressed. Then, suddenly, overcome by an unaccountable sadness, she indulged in a thing she rarely let herself do. She began to cry.

When the professor asked her to marry him, that late spring morning of her thirty-second year, all these incidents, from their different times in her past, came simultaneously back to her. They seemed to stretch out before her, brightly coloured materials on a market stall. She had the feeling that within a few years this stall would be dismantled: she would have to get up and go elsewhere with nothing to show for herself except for these old remnants of the past. So far, all signs of hope had been false alarms. Disillusioned still further, could she guarantee not to become bitter, bleak, introvert and hopeless?

Here the professor was offering an alternative – a life she had never imagined, hoped for or wanted. But she was cursed with a mind that fell into pictures at any suggestion. With the professor's question in the air, she at once began to imagine her life with him. An easy, shaggy life it would be: music, musical friends – for the most part much older than Virginia – moving about the country listening to him lecture, learning from him, laughing with him, knowing when to leave him to his taciturn moods. He would be kind, gentle, thoughtful: remembering through her youth his first wife, perhaps. Maybe they would have a child to replace Gretta.

Then Virginia thought of her nine years of teaching: there would be no more school, no more queuing for the bus in the rain, dissecting dandelions, or setting the Monday painting composition. She would forget the average times of Mr Fly's runs to the station, and the annoyance of Mrs Fly's way of chipping at her egg. Maybe even the dreaded man with the black moustache would leave her in peace once she had a husband.

Aware of all these things, Virginia opened her eyes. The professor had waited a long time, very patiently. He looked neither hopeful nor pessimistic, but a little solemn.

'Thank you, Professor,' said Virginia. 'I would like to be your wife.' The professor scooped up one of her hands in his and put it to his mouth. He kissed it.

'For God's sake, you can't go on calling me Professor now.' He was almost smiling.

'That's how I shall always think of you.'

'Whatever you like, for heaven's sake.' He lowered his head on to her knee. Virginia touched the coarse, grey hair. Strange: she had never thought of touching it before: never imagined it or desired it. Why did it smell slightly resinous, like pine trees? 'I think it could be a good thing. What do you think?'

'Excellent.' Virginia had heard her own voice so many times, say 'excellent' in that precise way. Red chalk at the end of an essay. 'Excellent, Louise, Mary, Sarah, Jemima . . .' Excellent. But the professor didn't seem to notice. He raised his head again.

'We will go in for no vulgar celebrations,' he said. 'Do you agree?'

'Absolutely.' If they went on agreeing as easily as this for the rest of their lives, what happiness.

'What is the need? All this call for celebration, cracking of champagne bottles. Unless, that is, you think I am being mean?'

'Of course not.' Virginia laughed.

'At some time we will have to get down to the unromantic business of making plans.'

'Perhaps we could marry at the end of the summer term?' suggested Virginia. 'It begins in two days' time.'

'There is no hurry. We have both waited so many years.' He stroked her hand. 'I was always inarticulate on the subject of love, Virginia Fly, particularly if I meant it. And now I am quite out of practice, as you can see. But you may be sure I would not have asked you to be my wife had not my heart been in it. I cannot guarantee to be an ideal husband – my God, I'm so old for a start . . .'

He sat quite still, for a moment, waiting, and then Virginia flung herself into his arms. They rubbed their cheeks, their heads together: swayed back and forth, and murmured things. Then the professor remembered the business of the day: he had to give a lecture in Reading, and time was getting on. Virginia was forced to put back on her new clothes, which reminded her briefly of the horrors of the night before. The professor observed her with affection as she stood in his warm untidy room, a pale, thin creature savaged by the bright colours she wore.

'Beautiful, but out of character,' he murmured. 'I liked best your governess look. That is what I am used to. Now, I must hurry. Let me take you to your train.'

He insisted, now that she was to be his wife, on buying her a first-class ticket. At the barrier, he bowed to her, out of habit, kissed her on the forehead, and hurried away to his lecture. Alone in the carriage, Virginia began to wonder what she had done.

Chapter 10

The summer term began. With a small band of amethysts and pearls round her finger, Virginia's status was heightened in the eyes of her pupils. They had never been more obedient, willing, friendly. Every Monday the painting composition turned into The Wedding Day – pink-faced brides awash with white poster paint dresses, doll-like bridesmaids carrying bunches of flowers tall as themselves, red-trousered grooms waving stunted arms and splitting their faces with grins.

At break times the children whispered in corners, pooled their money, added and re-added, planning The Present. Nature lessons turned into questions on the facts of human life, a subject which seemed to stimulate them far more than the ways of the amoeba.

'Miss Fly, how soon will you be getting a baby after you come out of the church?'

'Will you like sleeping in the same bed as your husband even when he's very new?'

'Will you think of us sometimes even when he's kissing you?'

Virginia answered their questions as well as she could. Flattered by their interest, she had never regarded them with more affection. The image of them, heads bent low over books, sun shining on bare arms, stamped itself on her mind. She would miss them. She would miss, too, the classroom: its familiar chipped paint, dented linoleum floor, the wall of paintings, the shelf of rough clay models, the chorus of squeaking chairs, the wild flowers and specimen leaves and the dreadful poster of Stone Age Man in England, presented by one of the school governors. This room had been her refuge for nine years, the place she had felt most safe, most in command. To leave it for ever would be a wrench, chilly, difficult.

Virginia and the professor, in these last few weeks before marriage, settled down to some sort of a routine. On Tuesday evenings Virginia would go to London to see him. Usually they would go to a concert or a theatre, have dinner, and Virginia would catch the last train home. On Saturday afternoons the professor would come to Acacia Avenue, spend the night, and return home on Sunday after tea. On such occasions Mrs Fly allowed them little time alone together, such was her enthusiasm to hear exhaustive details about their future. The professor found her tiresome almost beyond endurance, but for Virginia's sake remained infinitely polite and courteous, thus locking himself more firmly in her claustrophobic affection.

When they had time, they made plans. One afternoon, when Mrs Fly was out on one of her little errands, the professor let himself into Virginia's bedroom. She was on her knees, turning out cupboards. The professor lowered himself on to the candlewick bedspread. Virginia, glancing at him, was aware of the difference between him and the man she had always imagined would storm her window and possess her. With an effort, she cast such stupid thoughts aside, and turned to a pile of concert programmes.

'Ah! You have kept all those.' The discovery of her hoard seemed significant to the professor.

'Yes. I throw practically nothing away.' She remembered Charlie's letters and photograph flaring in the boiler.

'It must be an omen. They must have meant something to you.' It was difficult to tell if the professor was teasing.

'They reminded me of all the things we've been to hear.'

'Together.'

'Together,' Virginia agreed. He was so easy to please, the professor, sometimes.

'Come here a moment.' Virginia went towards him on her knees. He put his arm on her shoulder. 'I think we should buy ourselves a cottage in the Welsh mountains for weekends and holidays and our old age. Would you like that?'

Virginia's spirits rose. She hugged the professor's knee. 'Please let's do that.' Water from their own well, perhaps. Thick, thick walls and real fires. Those views. Snowed up Christmas. Books, walks, sun, music, peace. Pictures again, pleasing pictures.

'Very well, we will set about it. On our honeymoon we will drive around looking till we find something.' The professor, rewarded by her reaction, was finding it hard to control his voice.

'That would be really lovely. I shall look forward to that.' Virginia's eyes came near to shining. The professor kneaded one of her ears and felt the blush rising on her cheek.

'You look quite happy. Are you happy?'

'Of course.'

'You don't want to change your mind?'

'Sometimes you are quite absurd, Professor.'

'Oh, Virginia Fly.' He felt old man's tears pricking at his eyes. They sat in silence for a while.

Then Mrs Fly returned and began calling them. Determined to keep their new plan from her, lest it should be in some way undermined by her inevitable doubts, they went down to join her for tea.

But later that week, alone in the staff-room during a free

period before lunch, Virginia abandoned correcting English essays and wrote her first letter to the professor. She wrote fast and easily, her hand firm, pinpricks of sweat on her nose.

My Dearest Dear Professor – Please think of the other morning when you asked me to marry you as a dream which didn't really happen. Because I can't ever marry you. Your affection swayed me when I was low: I am fond of you and I enjoy being with you and you seemed – forgive my cruelty here – to be something I could clutch to. I said yes hardly knowing what I was doing. It was wrong of me, unforgivable of me, and I ask you if you can forgive me. But I cannot marry you because you see I don't love you in the way that I should love someone with whom I'm going to spend the rest of my life. You don't fill me with a terrible passion that is impossible to live without. I don't feel sick and dizzy in your presence. I don't miss you enough when you're not there. I don't feel you are my whole life. You don't shake my foundations. I have a million doubts. There, clumsy as ever, I am. Hurting, surely, but only in order to make you believe that I'm serious, to make you believe it will be a disaster for both of us if we go through with it.

I am sorry. Yours, Virginia Fly.

With a calm determination she sealed the envelope, addressed it, stamped it. She would walk to the village now and post it, to make sure it arrived in the morning. But on her way down the passage the bell rang. She was on lunch duty. There was no time. She put her letter in the bag.

At lunch she was aware of feeling sick. The noise of clattering plates and a couple of hundred high voices jarred on her ears with a freshness which reminded her of the first time she had dined in this echoing hall nine years ago. The lump of semolina with its eye of strawberry jam blurred before her eyes.

'Miss Fly, are you all right?' Damn the child.

'Fine, thank you.' Send the letter, and there would be years and years more semolina, wouldn't there?

As soon as grace was over, she slipped round to the dustbins at the back door, tore the letter into innumerable small pieces, and threw it away.

For Mrs Thompson, Virginia's engagement was the culmination of the happiest spring she could remember since Bill died. As other people fester on regret at some past action in their lives, Mrs Thompson daily thrived on self-congratulation: writing to Virginia Fly had been the most rewarding gesture she had made in years. True, it hadn't turned out quite as she had expected: it was Mrs Fly who had become her great friend rather than Virginia. But that was only to be expected, due to the generation gap. Still, she was very fond of Virginia: she was such a nice, quiet, sensible girl, with something of a humorous eye. The kind of daughter she would have liked to have had herself. The kind of girl you could understand – not like most of the younger generation to-day, with their scruffy clothes and funny moods. The kind of girl who needed a bit of protection and advice as to the ways of this wicked world – Mrs Thompson could help her there, and would see to it as far as she could that Virginia came to no harm. It was a pity that the Ulick Brand plan hadn't worked out: he had seemed such a nice, well-off young man. Mrs Thompson would have liked to have taken credit for the match. Still, the professor was probably altogether more suitable. Older men were steadier. More trustworthy. Less energy to go gallivanting about. In all, a better bet. Besides, as Mrs Thompson joked to Virginia with amazing regularity, she quite fancied the professor herself. That lovely thick grey hair and those sensitive hands (she always noticed hands). You could tell he was a wonderful pianist.

If anything, Virginia's engagement brought Mrs Thompson and Mrs Fly even closer together. There was so much to discuss, so much about which to give their invaluable advice. They found in each other a reflection of their own enthusiasm: they found the warmth of agreement and the pleasure of mutual, rosy tinted reminiscence. Indulging in these things meant the necessity of being together a great deal: Mrs Thompson came down to Acacia Avenue most weekends now, often staying on for Monday night and only, with reluctance, dragging herself back to London on Tuesday to keep her date with Mrs Baxter. Mrs Fly would have been delighted for her to stay the whole week.

In fact, at this happy time, Mrs Thompson had only one real problem: Mrs Baxter.

Mrs Baxter was jealous. Bright green, and it showed. Mrs Thompson, for her part, had done her best. No matter how great the wrench of leaving Acacia Avenue, she had always turned up on their regular Tuesday night. What's more, she had kept nothing from Mrs Baxter. She'd told her everything: she even persuaded Mrs Fly to send her an invitation to the wedding. Mrs Baxter took this in quite the wrong way.

'Huh! Expect me to go troll-olling along to the wedding of some fancy people I don't even know, do you? You can keep your charity to yourself.'

It was no good explaining. Mrs Baxter didn't want any explanations. She also didn't ever want to hear another word about the Flys, and made this clear to Mrs Thompson in no uncertain terms.

Mrs Thompson, as she later told Mrs Fly – who was very sympathetic about the whole situation – was very hurt. But, for old time's sake, she resolved to curb her tongue. For several weeks, as the result of a superhuman effort, she managed not to mention any one of them.

But the strain told upon her and, some Tuesday nights, when she and Mrs Baxter parted, she found herself in tears of frustration. It would have been so nice to ask Mrs Baxter's opinion about her new wedding hat, her dress, the colour of her bag and shoes . . . Friends, she reflected, sometimes asked too much of you. Still, she shouldn't complain. At least she *had* friends. For the first time for years she thanked God for her blessings, and when she rose from her knees she gave a little skip of pleasure. The day after to-morrow was Friday again, and meant another Surrey weekend.

One night, about six weeks before the end of term, Virginia had a dream about her black-moustached seducer. She woke trembling, sweating, weak and cold. Having thought he had left her for ever, his return terrified her. She lay writhing in the damp twisted sheets, watching the full moon cut into diamonds by the panes of her lattice window. She thought of the touch of the man's hand on her body, soothing her neck, cupping each breast in turn, and she stifled a scream in the pillow. Some time later, finally exhausted by frustrated desire, she succumbed to common sense, a defence she had always instilled into herself so hard throughout her life that it escaped her only momentarily in moments of crisis.

She got out of bed, put on her dressing-gown and lit the bedside lamp. She would write, finally, to the professor. Marriage, without the kind of passion she had just experienced, was not possible. There was no further choice. She would begin to wait once more. After all, she was used to waiting.

Dear Professor, *My Dear Professor*, she wrote in the red marking pen that happened to be beside her bed, *I am dreadfully sorry but we cannot cannot cannot go through with it. It would not be fair to either of us, especially to you. With all my heart*

173

I want to love you totally, but I can't. I want us to be delirious and wild and passionate – but we aren't like that, are we? We are marvellous friends and I know people tell you friendship is the best basis for marriage, but I do believe you must start with something else as well or even the friendship won't survive. It's a little different for you. You had, a long time ago, a perfect kind of love. You have had time to recover a bit, and I will be something different – secure and nice and friendly for your old age. But you see I never had that first bit. I have tried to love people, but it has always been fantasy, never the real thing. And I believe that must come to everyone at least once in a lifetime, even if one has to wait till one is fifty. Therefore I am afraid. What happens if I marry you, feeling like I do, settle for our compromise, and in years to come I fall in love with someone? Oh God, dear professor, that would be dreadful. Neither of us could ever want that to happen.

Here, trembling and feeling very cold again, she got up to shut the window. The sky was filling with summer dawn, veins of mercury in the clouds, the ugly lawn silvered with dew, the birds already alert and full of song.

'Virginia Fly, you're a fool,' she said out loud.

So please forgive me if I go from your life, which would be better than the possibility of destroying it. I can't tell you all this because I am a moral coward. I wish I could have written it better. With love and affection, Virginia Fly.

After that, Virginia slept till the sun was high and it was breakfast time.

Getting dressed, the perfection of the morning made itself felt even in her unimaginative room, and brightened the dull Surrey view outside. She couldn't help thinking of Wales: there, such a morning wouldn't be wasted. She would collect a warm egg for the professor's breakfast while he stoked up the fire, and then sit in the mountain sun all day with books she'd never had time to read.

Once more, Virginia found herself going down to the boiler. The shreds of her second letter to the professor, which she hadn't bothered to re-read, were devoured in a moment. The despair of the night was past. This morning she was all common sense.

The Wedding Day was the bright light on Mrs Fly's horizon. She found the joy of anticipation almost unbearable, and certainly something she couldn't keep to herself. Every morning Mr Fly and Virginia were subjected to new thoughts on the matter.

'Oh Ginny, before I forget to tell you – I was awake most of the night thinking about it, I can't think why it didn't come to us before – I've had a brainwave.' Mr Fly, controlling a sigh, picked up his paper. Mrs Fly tapped at her egg with a minuscule silver spoon. 'Ted, I think you should listen to this. I think you should take an interest. It's not every day your daughter gets married.' Mr Fly continued to read his paper.

'I am listening,' he said.

'I shall want your advice to prove it.' His wife took her first tiny sip of yolk. 'Well, it's this. Bridesmaids. On the subject of bridesmaids. Had you thought about them, Ginny?'

'Only that I wouldn't have any.'

'In the normal way I would agree with you, not having any young relations. But how about my brainwave? I thought: why not have all the girls in your class? There are twelve of them, aren't there? Imagine, they'd make quite a little train.'

Mr Fly spluttered, trying to suppress a laugh.

'Do be serious, Ted,' snapped his wife. 'You don't seem to be taking this wedding at all seriously. Now listen to this. I've got it all worked out. Twelve little bridesmaids, most of them quite pretty as far as I can remember from Speech Day. Wouldn't they look a sight? In lime, I thought. Lime would be lovely in July. And it's not a normal bridesmaid colour, is it? Lime Kate Greenaway dresses with little posies of stephanotis and gardenias, and bonnets on their heads trimmed with the same flowers. What do you think?'

There was a long pause. Then:

'Don't ask me,' said Mr Fly, getting up. 'I thought ordering the champagne was to be my only responsibility.' He went to the door. This irritated his wife.

'Where are you going?'

'Work.'

'But you haven't finished your toast.'

'I know.'

'But you usually do.'

'This morning, I don't want to.' For the first time that she could recall in forty years her husband slammed the door. She gave a small shudder.

'Oh dear, I don't know what's the matter with him.'

'You can't expect him to be interested in dress-making details,' said Virginia. 'Besides, the wedding has been the sole topic of conversation for six weeks now. Couldn't we talk about something to interest Father, for once? No wonder he's resentful.'

Mrs Fly sniffed.

'I can see whose side you're on,' she said. Deflated, she scooped up the small threads of egg yolk which, in spite of all her careful management, had dribbled down the side of the shell. 'Well, what do you think about my idea?'

'No,' said Virginia, firmly. 'Absolutely no. I'm sorry, but I hate lime and twelve schoolchildren bridesmaids would be totally absurd.'

Rarely did Virginia speak so sharply to her mother. Mrs Fly's eyes brimmed with tears.

'I don't think you can realise, Ginny,' she said, her voice a-quiver, 'exactly what a wedding means to the bride's mother.'

'Probably not,' said Virginia, still hard. 'And I don't think *you* realise that the trappings are not the important part. If the professor and I had our way, we'd be married in a Northern registry office with *no one*, *no* relations there.' Mrs Fly stood up quickly, grasping the edges of the table cloth with her shaky hands.

'You can't mean what you're saying, child,' she shouted. 'After all these years of saying your prayers and you don't want to be married before God? You can't mean it – '

'I do,' Virginia shouted back, sickened by her mother's tears. 'You'd better go and tell Mrs Thompson, and see what she has to say about it.'

Virginia left the room, slamming the door like her father. She always reacted badly to scenes. Her hands were shaking by now, and she was sweating under the arms. At this moment, she realised, she and her mother had never been farther apart.

Not far along the road she was stopped by her father in his mini shooting brake.

'Ginny? I'll give you a lift.'

'Father! What are you doing here?'

'Just driving around, you know. Filling in time. I made myself a trifle early.' He winked. When she was in the car he said: 'I'm sorry I went off like that. I just thought if I heard another word about bridesmaids' dresses . . . Your mother's a little overwrought. I don't blame her, of course.' He smiled. 'Do you happen to know if Mrs Thompson is coming down again this weekend?'

'I believe she is.' Virginia watched her father's face. A muscle clenched in his neck. He spoke tightly.

'I have a feeling, once you've gone, Ginny, she'll be down most weekends. Still, that man near Hastings, you know, the one I got the lawn mower from, he's become quite a friend of mine. He's asked me over any time. Said I could go any time I liked, and he'll take me gliding. I quite fancy a bit of floating about the skies. Maybe I'll go over there on Saturday.' This was the first time he had mentioned either his new friendship or his new hobby.

'That will be nice,' said Virginia, pleased: and then suddenly, all in a rush, 'and you will come to us any time you like won't you? To London or Wales? Any time Mrs Thompson overdoes it?' Mr Fly laughed.

'I wouldn't want to inflict myself upon you, Ginny.'

'You'd never be doing that.'

'Well, I dare say, average traffic, I could make it up to you in no time at all.'

He left her near the school. Driving off, sitting very upright, hands clasped on the wheel cautiously as a learner, he decided not to take the risk of waving. Virginia watched till his carefully polished car was out of sight. She wondered about his old age.

Speech Day was on the last day of term. The professor, having been invited by the headmistress herself, agreed to come, after much persuasion. He made an effort for the occasion: pressed suit, clean shirt, and new tie. Remarkably distinguished, he looked, Virginia thought with pride.

As was the case of all members of staff who left after years of hard and devoted service, effulgent tributes were paid to Virginia. She sat, disbelieving, as words of praise were sent forth in short, trembling speeches by girls with sweating hands. The headmistress wished her well in her marriage and hoped she would come back and visit the school often. A girl from her own class, curtsying, suddenly nervous, presented her with a huge bunch of yellow roses. Finally, the whole school gave three cheers for Miss Fly. Down below, in the hall, the professor laughed and clapped in the front row, proud of her. She muttered thanks, and smiled till her face ached. 'I'm overwhelmed, what *can* I say?' It was all insanity.

A violent chord on the piano lopped off the emotion of the moment. The whole school stood, paused, then crashed into 'Jerusalem'. Then they marched out, familiar thud of feet, last time in the familiar hall, all those beautiful straight backs, on the platform Miss Graham's petticoat showing as usual . . .

'It's a wonder you're not bloody crying at it all,' whispered Mr Bluett, making her smile a proper smile at last.

Later, she took the professor to her classroom. There he was a triumph. He met every pupil, shook each one by the hand, examined and commented on twenty-four paintings of his own wedding. The children presented him and Virginia with their present, wrapped in paper painted by themselves. A carriage clock, long saved for. The professor's delight enchanted them: they crowded round him, touching him, calling for his attention, getting to know as quickly as they could the man who was taking their teacher away.

All the farewells over, the professor picked up Virginia's small case. In it she had put the things that had accumulated in her desk over the years. She unpinned and packed the wedding paintings; she took the clay ashtrays, pressed butterflies and flowers that her pupils, on various private occasions, had given her during the term. Finally, she rubbed out the end of term notices from the blackboard, and they left the empty classroom.

'I feel a bastard taking you away from them,' said the professor. Virginia laughed. Now it was over, now they were out of the gates, she felt better.

'You were marvellous with them,' she said. 'You didn't let me down.'

'You wait, my love, you wait,' he joked. 'My God, marriage is a state of perpetual crisis, didn't you know

179

that? Sometimes one is not always strong enough to deal with it in the best way.' He saw a look of fear flinch in Virginia's eyes. 'No – for heaven's sake. I was exaggerating. With you, it will all be calm and peaceful. At least, mostly. Won't it?'

'I hope so.' said Virginia.

Before the train left, in the carriage, the professor told her he loved her considerably more this afternoon, if that was possible. Other people's appreciation of her had added to his own. He was impatient for the week they had left to go by.

'I want you, my love,' he said, 'profoundly.'

Nevertheless, when his train had gone, Virginia went to the station waiting-room and began him one more letter.

Oh my dear love – we can't, we can't, we can't. I don't believe we should . . .

But she knew that there was no point in going on, that she would never send it.

Instead of taking the bus, she walked home. On the way she planned her escape: London to-night by train. The Golden Arrow to Paris – her passport was in order. Then, the first train south. On to Italy, Greece, Turkey. She had saved enough money. She would send postcards to say no one was to worry. The professor would forget her. In a year, she might return. Find a new life. If she had the courage to carry out this decision, she might be rewarded.

At home she found her mother, still in her Speech Day hat, in the kitchen making curry.

'I'm doing your father's favourite,' she explained, in a more subdued tone than she had used for several weeks. 'Poor Ted. I don't know what's wrong with him. He's been quite down, not at all himself lately. When they gave you those flowers and cheered you like that he became quite tearful. I've never seen him like that before. So I thought he'd like a curry again. I haven't had much time lately, have I? – Here, would you peel me a few apples?'

Virginia went obediently to the sink. She wondered at what point during the evening she could escape to get her things together, and how she would word the letter that explained her departure.

The day of the wedding was, as Mr Fly pointed out, a very average day for mid-July. The sky was a taut blue, and a few spongy white clouds, hesitant to cross the sun's face and cast shadows on the proceedings, hovered above the line of trees. The air smelt of flowers – not from the flower beds, which were nothing but thin lines of crumbled grey earth this year, due to Mr Fly's numerous weekend visits to the new friend in Hastings, but from the pedestal vases feathered with great blooms that stood snootily in the marquee. This contraption had been put up some nights before. Virginia resented its presence. It meant that from her bedroom she could no longer see the garden. The tent's canvas spine and sloping sides blotted out the familiar view. And in the last few days she had felt a desperate need for familiarity.

But, everywhere, it had almost disappeared. The sense of the strangeness of the house increased from day to day, culminating in the morning of the wedding. The dining-room, at breakfast, was darkened by the marquee. Most of the furniture had been moved out of the sitting-room. The hall and kitchen smelt of cheese fingers. Mrs Fly wore an apron, slippers, and no stockings while she busied about giving orders to Mrs Thompson. Men in white coats came in and out carrying trays of *petits fours*. Mr Fly wandered up and down the side of the marquee, testing the guy ropes with both hands. He expressed a sudden and unusual concern about the strips of gritty earth that he called his flower beds: hoped too many people wouldn't stand upon them. Mrs Fly's hopes were that Caroline would manage to come, for Virginia's sake, and the caterers had spelt the professor's name correctly on the cake. Virginia, unable to think of anything useful to do, counted the bridge rolls smeared with mashed sardine.

Mid-morning, she found a small, fat, bald-headed man looking bewildered in the hall. He introduced himself: Inigo Schrub, best man. Of course. Virginia remembered him from their brief meeting at the professor's lecture. He had studied music with Hans in Vienna. Now, he was first violin in a Midland orchestra. He smiled, his eyes magnifying uncannily behind his thick glasses.

'I wondered – I don't really know my duties – but would it be in order to take the bride for a drink?'

Virginia accepted gratefully. Anything to get out of the house.

They walked a quarter of a mile to the nearest pub. Inigo seemed slightly out of breath: walking and talking at the same time was not easy for him.

'Hans, my old friend, is a lucky man indeed,' he gasped. 'He deserves so delicious a woman. He deserves after all these years an admirable wife.'

'Then he shouldn't be marrying me,' Virginia heard herself saying. 'I'm not at all the right person for him. I'll be a dreadful wife. I'm too – set in my ways. I can't explain. I just know we're making a mistake.' For a fleeting moment she had a feeling this stranger would understand, even rescue her. 'Can't you tell him, even now? You're his best friend. It's not too late. We could put it off. We shouldn't go through with it. Really.'

'My dear girl, pre-wedding nerves. I know just how you feel.' He patted her arm, a million miles away. 'What you need is a drink. It's always the bride who suffers before the wedding. Here, what shall I get you?'

As she didn't answer, he bought her brandy and they sat at a tin table under a small awning advertising beer.

'There, now, you look very pale. You shouldn't have worked yourself up into such a state.' A friendly, caricature grandfather, he was. 'Hans wouldn't make a decision about marriage unless he knew what he was doing.'

'He knows what *he's* doing. He doesn't know what *I'm* doing, that's the point,' Virginia's voice was very high.

'My dear Virginia, you are very young.'

'I'm not.'

'Compared with Hans.'

'Oh, compared with Hans, I suppose. But what has that to do with anything?' She sighed, suddenly very weary. Inigo, completely at loss how to help her, drummed his knuckles on the tin table top.

'It will work out all right, you'll see. It's the shock of the plunge, I expect, after waiting some years of your life. You know how reality is. It always shatters illusion in the most cruel way. In a most devastatingly cruel way.' He shook his large round head from side to side. Balls of sweat ran from his temples to his puffed out cheeks. 'But that is what we're here for. That is our function – to live with the reality and bury the dreams, no matter how long we've lived with *them* . . . There, I'm preaching. I apologise.'

'I'm sorry,' said Virginia, shyly, ashamed. 'I'm being very hysterical. Put it down to nerves, as you said. Nonetheless,' she added, then paused for a moment. 'Nonetheless, I'm convinced I'm doing the wrong thing.'

'My dear girl, no more of this talk.' Inigo sounded almost impatient, then noticed her eyes. 'Why are you appealing to me? How can *I* help you? The marriage is in two hours. You must think of my friend Hans. Don't you think that to let him down now would be a grave injustice?'

Virginia raised her head and smiled at him, self-mockingly.

'Hans, luckily, is not very concerned with my past. I

don't think he knows or cares that I have never loved anyone. He doesn't know that I was raped by an American penfriend, for example, or went to bed with a man I had great stupid hopes for, only to be turned out by his wife.'

Inigo Schrub coughed, confused. The copper colour of his face deepened.

'These are dramatic situations . . .' His voice trailed away. Virginia was no longer listening.

'You wait till you see my wedding dress,' she was saying. 'Funny, but even over that I gave in in the end. It was always easier, for peace and quiet, not to resist my mother. Not to argue.

'My father and I always supported each other,' she went on, 'but he had these ridiculously high hopes for me. I never won anything at school, except for art. It would have made him the happiest man in the world if I'd been the sort of girl who won prizes. I let him down over and over again. He was brave about it, but disappointed. So when he suggested I should become a teacher, I agreed. I didn't want to. I wanted to paint. But my decision pleased him so much, I couldn't go back on it. He deserved something, didn't he? It wasn't such a dreadful sacrifice, after all his support. It was easier.

'Believe me,' she added, 'I must have been an awful child. Goody Goody they called me at school. Goody Ginny Goody. I used to make devilish plans to provoke them into liking me. They all failed . . Perhaps I was shy and awkward, more so than I realised. I know I was plain. Anyhow, I gave up a certain amount of hope.'

'You could never have been plain,' interrupted Inigo Schrub. The top of the table was warm under Virginia's flattened palms. She twitched one of her hands slightly, so that the shaft of sun on her knuckles was forced to slide down the long slopes of her fingers.

'Instead, I settled for anticipation,' she went on. 'Much

better. You can thrive, you know, anticipating on small things you're sure will happen. That's far less gloomy than hoping for bigger things that may never come about.' Virginia spoke so softly that Inigo Schrub had to bend his head to hear. She narrowed her eyes. The midday sun was hard.

'You can watch yourself from a long way off, for many years – maybe all your life,' she continued. 'You can see your pathetic gestures, know what you are doing wrong. And yet you're powerless to change your actions. You may hate yourself for your inability, but still you remain powerless.'

'You watch yourself become crushed, then,' observed Inigo. He signalled for more drinks. Virginia's glass had been empty for some time.

'Quite,' she agreed, seeming to realise his presence again, 'though in my case I *fitted in*, rather than became crushed. Fitting in is easy, once you have the knack. It becomes the simplest way of life. People like you for it. You're no trouble. But they don't love you for it.'

'Then you will be submerged.' Inigo Schrub suddenly banged his fist on the table top, making it echo. 'You have no right to watch yourself drown.'

'I have little alternative, Mr Schrub. I have no pity for myself, only a certain dread for our future, the professor's and mine.'

Inigo's body, almost as wide as the table top, seemed to have sunk down.

'You will resist, believe me,' he said. Virginia drank her second brandy with thirst.

'I doubt my resistance,' she said.

'If our whole life were not cast about with such doubts, then certainty itself would be of no value. As it is, believe me, please, you can be certain of Hans's devotion to you. And don't deride yourself too far. You have such affection to give . . .' He petered out once more, embarrassing himself by his display of conviction. To detract from his confusion, he looked at his watch and suggested they should go. After all, there was no more to say.

On the way back, what with the sun and the brandy, and Inigo's guttural voice, so similar to the professor's, and his fat supporting arm, Virginia felt quite strong.

She and Inigo joked about the preposterous events of the afternoon ahead, and even laughed.

After an attempt to eat a small lunch – no one tried very hard – Mr and Mrs Fly, Mrs Thompson (who had installed herself a week before to help) and Virginia went to their separate rooms, watches synchronised.

Virginia sat on her bed wondering what to do first. Under the candlewick bedspread she could feel the squares of folded blankets: her bed as it used to be no longer. It was very hot in the room, in spite of two open windows. Breezeless. Through the canvas of the marquee came the voices of people shouting orders.

Her case was packed, open. Only the things for her face and hair on the dressing-table. The dress – a horrible compromise of a dress – hung outside the cupboard. Virginia had refused the stark white, long satin her mother had longed for. But she had eventually agreed not to wear floppy crêpe of brightly coloured flowers. The compromise was a pink taffeta thing ('salmon's blush,' Mrs Thompson called it, meaning it as a compliment) of indeterminate shape. In a hundred years' time, found in an attic, it would be hard to place the decade it belonged to. Pink satin shoes to match, toes demurely touching under the cupboard. And the hat, shimmering on its stand: a bundle of pink flowers whose petals sprouted forth a paler pink veil. If it hadn't been so awful, it would have been funny, Virginia thought.

A knock on the door. Mrs Fly and Mrs Thompson, together. Mrs Thompson seemed to have powdered her face with flour. Blue feathers from her head cascaded down one cheek. Already they were becoming floury. Mrs Fly was a shock of emerald green. Nylon gloves covered her elbows, each one done up with fifty pearl buttons. The wedges of her arms, between the top of her violent gloves and capped sleeves, were rough with nervous goose pimples. Mascara and lipstick, both smudged, blurred her mouth and eyes.

They stood, side by side, in the door.

'Oh, Ginny. Not ready yet?' Mrs Fly took a small step forward. 'Your father's expecting you down in twenty minutes. Don't keep him waiting, will you?' She paused. 'May I kiss you?'

Virginia stood.

'If you like,' she said. Mrs Thompson, too, took her chance to peck at the offered cheek. They both patted her, said stupid things in difficult voices, and left.

Alone again, Virginia sat at her dressing-table and brushed her hair. The curls which had been put in yesterday had fallen out over night, leaving it straggly with ill-formed waves. Her face was chalky white. She burnished it with rouge, and greased her dry lips to make them shine.

Dressed, she looked at herself in the small mirror once more. The pink bodice of her dress shone up into her translucent face. It caused a nasty reflection. The petal hat rested uneasily and uncomfortably on her disappointing hair, and the satin shoes already hurt her feet.

With a calm hand, quite resigned, she pulled the salmon veil down over her face. She thought, suddenly, of Inigo Schrub.

'Virginia Fly is drowning,' she said to herself, out loud. She dabbed her wrists with scent, ran both hands very fast along the candlewick bedspread, so that they were left tingling for several moments, and went to the door.

Downstairs, her father, in hired morning suit, paced up and down the cheese-straw smelling hall. At the sight of her on the stairs he smiled. Neither of them spoke.

In the large black hired car, its seats covered in soft material, the air smelt of a previous hirer's cigar. There was a space of grey seat between them; Mr Fly laid his hand there. Virginia covered it with hers. It felt strangely different – curiously smooth. Looking down, her glance hidden by her veil, Virginia saw her father had shaved his knuckles. Quickly, she withdrew her hand.

They drove to the church with appalling slowness.

'I've been averaging it out, several evenings this week, in the mini, so as I could tell the driver exactly how long . . .' Mr Fly began. His voice petered out. He put out a clenched knuckle as if to tap the window that divided them from the driver, but withdrew it.

At the gates of the Victorian church, its red brick a sour colour in the vivid sun, a small crowd craned and murmured. Stepping from the car, Virginia felt very cold. Her father supported her with shaking hand. They took small steps up the bright pathway. Virginia was conscious that her ankle bones clacked together.

They reached the porch of the church, stony cool and dark after the sun. Through the open door, they could see the multi-coloured litter of hats and backs fixed to the pews. Compelled by some strange instinct – a compliment to past closeness, perhaps – a mass of small heads at once strained round to try to see Virginia. All my pupils, she thought. The words went through her head like beads. Then, breaking the spell, she saw her mother raise her arm to point out something to Mrs Thompson. The spine of pearl buttons flashed on her dreadful green glove.

At the altar, stiff waxy flowers were arranged top-heavily on pedestals, their pale petals chequered with garish lights from the stained-glass window. Beside, and almost under one of them, Inigo Schrub, his fat back strained into a small black coat, stood to attention. The professor's grey head was lowered towards his. He whispered something. But the best man did not respond. On one of his trouser legs his fingers drummed in time to the ponderous Bach.

When the music came to an end, at some sign invisible to Virginia, the congregation rose with a unanimous clatter strangely noisy for people in such light summer things. For one moment they were silent. Virginia's hand crept to the stomach of her dress. Protected by her bouquet of salmon pink carnations cast in fern, she scratched.

Love Divine, all loves excelling,
Joy of Heav'n, to earth come down . . .

The hymn had begun. Faces turned. Singing mouths paused, open, as the eyes looked. Virginia felt herself move. Suddenly she was in the aisle, her father beside her. Within a few paces, Mr Fly found himself out of step. Thus, in uneasy tandem, they approached the hideous altar where the professor waited for Virginia to become his wife.

LAND GIRLS

Angela Huth

'Piquant, witty and entertaining'
Tatler

The West Country in wartime, and the land girls are gathering on
the farm of John and Faith Lawrence.

Prue, a man-eating hairdresser from Manchester; Ag, a cerebral
Cambridge undergraduate; and Stella, a dreamy Surrey girl stunted
by love: three very different women, from very different back-
grounds, who find themselves thrown together, sharing an
attic bedroom and laying the foundations for a friendship that
will last a lifetime.

'Angela Huth's riveting novel ... is evocative and entertaining'
Mail on Sunday

'It had me in its grip and I couldn't rest until the final page ... It is
satisfying and rare to read a book whose characters are dealt the
fates we feel they deserve ... A beautifully spun tale that absorbs
without the need to address "issues"'
Literary Review

'A good story, told with wit and a keen observation of detail'
Times Literary Supplement

Abacus
0 349 10601 0

NOWHERE GIRL

Angela Huth

'A first-class writer'
Sunday Telegraph

Estranged from her second husband Jonathan, Clare Lyall is less
sure than ever about the role men should play in her life.

Her first husband, Richard, was much older than her, and his
casual disregard for youth gradually hardened into indifference.
And Jonathan, if anything, was too easy - too attentive, too
concerned, and just a little too pedantic.

So when she meets Joshua Heron at a party, the offbeat Clare
isn't exactly thirsting for love. But she *is* mildly impressed when
Joshua stubs his cigarette out on his thumb, and swayed still
further by the advice of her new friend, the indomitable Mrs Fox.
'Take a lover,' she says, 'it's better to have a lover when you're
young than neurosis when you're old ...'

Gentle, wistful and wry, *Nowhere Girl* is a beautifully
controlled love story from the acclaimed author of
Invitation to the Married Life.

'There is a very strong case for Huth replacing Jane Austen on
the school syllabus'
Sunday Times

Abacus

☐ Invitation to the Married Life	Angela Huth	£6.99
☐ Land Girls	Angela Huth	£6.99
☐ Nowhere Girl	Angela Huth	£6.99
☐ South of the Lights	Angela Huth	£6.99
☐ Going into a Dark House	Jane Gardam	£5.99
☐ Charms for the Easy Life	Kaye Gibbons	£5.99

Abacus now offers an exciting range of quality titles by both established and new authors. All of the books in this series are available from:

Little, Brown and Company (UK),
P.O. Box 11,
Falmouth,
Cornwall TR10 9EN.

Alternatively you may fax your order to the above address.
Fax No: 01326 317444
Telephone No: 01326 317200
E-mail: books@barni.avel.co.uk

Payments can be made as follows: cheque, postal order (payable to Little, Brown and Company) or by credit cards, Visa/Access. Do not send cash or currency. UK customers and B.F.P.O. please allow £1.00 for postage and packing for the first book, plus 50p for the second book, plus 30p for each additional book up to a maximum charge of £3.00 (7 books plus).

Overseas customers including Ireland, please allow £2.00 for the first book plus £1.00 for the second book, plus 50p for each additional book.

NAME (Block Letters) ....

....

ADDRESS ....

....

....

☐ I enclose my remittance for ....
☐ I wish to pay by Access/Visa Card

Number ☐☐☐☐☐☐☐☐☐☐☐☐☐☐☐☐☐☐

Card Expiry Date ☐☐☐☐